ELLIS ISLAND & OTHER STORIES

"His eye is precise and his spirit is compassionate, and when we finish the stories we have been rewarded, once more, with that astonishing catalyst of art."
—*The Chicago Tribune*

"Helprin creates strange, magical worlds. His rich textures alone would be enough to delight a reader . . . wonderful stories, richly plotted, inventive . . . moving without becoming sentimental, humorous without being cute . . ."
—*The Washington Post*

"Maybe it's just youthful energy or luck. But I don't think so. I think it's genius. . . . *Ellis Island* ascends to the peak of literary achievement."
—*The Boston Globe*

"The words . . . beg to be read aloud. . . . Through the humor, the beauty, the sheer delight of Helprin's creations shines a reverence for life, a gentle faith in the rejuvenation of the spirit."
—*Houston Chronicle*

"Helprin's prose looses the mind from its moorings and endows the senses with an almost painful clarity. . . . The title story, 'Ellis Island,' is a marvelous blend of pathos and humor."
—*The Kansas City Star*

ELLIS ISLAND
& Other Stories

Mark Helprin

A LAUREL/SEYMOUR LAWRENCE BOOK

Published by
Dell Publishing Co., Inc.
1 Dag Hammarskjold Plaza
New York, New York 10017

"The Schreuderspitze," "Letters from the *Samantha*," "Martin Bayer," "A Vermont Tale," "Tamar," and "Ellis Island" first appeared in *The New Yorker;* "Palais de Justice" in *The Real Paper;* and "A Room of Frail Dancers" in *Moment.*

For information address
Delacorte Press/Seymour Lawrence, New York, New York

Laurel ® TM 674623, Dell Publishing Co., Inc.

ISBN: 0-440-32204-9

Reprinted by arrangement with
Delacorte Press/Seymour Lawrence.
Printed in the United States of America
Three Previous Delta Printings
Second Laurel printing—June 1984

FOR LISA

Contents

The
Schreuderspitze

In Munich are many men who look like weasels. Whether by genetic accident, meticulous crossbreeding, an early and puzzling migration, coincidence, or a reason that we do not know, they exist in great numbers. Remarkably, they accentuate this unfortunate tendency by wearing mustaches, Alpine hats, and tweed. A man who resembles a rodent should never wear tweed.

One of these men, a commercial photographer named Franzen, had cause to be exceedingly happy. "Herr Wallich has disappeared," he said to Huebner, his supplier of paper and chemicals. "You needn't bother to send him bills. Just send them to the police. The police, you realize, were here on two separate occasions!"

"If the two occasions on which the police have been here had not been separate, Herr Franzen, they would have been here only once."

"What do you mean? Don't toy with me. I have no time for semantics. In view of the fact that I knew Wallich at school, and professionally, they sought my opinion on his disappearance. They wrote down everything I said, but I do not think that they will find him. He left his studio on the Neuhausstrasse just as it was when he was working, and the landlord has put a lien on the equipment. Let me tell you that he had some fine equipment—very fine. But he was not such a great photographer. He didn't have that killer's instinct. He was clearly not a hunter. His canine teeth were poorly developed; not like these," said Franzen, baring his canine teeth in a smile which made him look like an idiot with a mouth of miniature castle towers.

"But I am curious about Wallich."

"So is everyone. So is everyone. This is my theory. Wallich was never any good at school. At best, he did only middling well. And it was not because he had hidden passions, or a special genius for some field outside the curriculum. He tried hard but found it difficult to grasp several subjects; for him, mathematics and physics were pure torture.

"As you know, he was not wealthy, and although he was a nice-looking fellow, he was terribly short. That inflicted upon him great scars—his confidence, I mean, because he had none. He could do things only gently. If he had to fight, he would fail. He was weak.

"For example, I will use the time when he and I were competing for the Heller account. This job meant a lot of money, and I was not about to lose. I went to the library and read all I could about turbine engines. What a bore! I took photographs of turbine blades and such things, and seeded them throughout my portfolio to make Herr Heller think that I had always been interested in turbines. Of course, I had not even known what they were. I thought that they were an Oriental hat. And now that I know them, I detest them.

"Naturally, I won. But do you know how Wallich approached the competition? He had some foolish ideas about mother-of-pearl nautiluses and other seashells. He wanted to show how shapes of things mechanical were echoes of shapes in nature. All very fine, but Herr Heller pointed out that if the public were to see photographs of mother-of-pearl shells contrasted with photographs of his engines, his engines would come out the worse. Wallich's photographs were very beautiful—the tones of white and silver were exceptional—but they were his undoing. In the end, he said, 'Perhaps, Herr Heller, you are right,' and lost the contract just like that.

"The thing that saved him was the prize for that picture he took in the Black Forest. You couldn't pick up a magazine in Germany and not see it. He obtained so many accounts that he began to do very well. But he was just not commercially-minded. He told me himself that he took only those assignments which pleased him. Mind you, his business volume was only about two-thirds of mine.

"My theory is that he could not take the competition, and the demands of his various clients. After his wife and son were killed in the motorcar crash, he dropped assignments one after another. I suppose he thought that as a bachelor he could live like a bohemian, on very little money, and therefore did not have to work more than half the time. I'm not saying that this was wrong. (Those accounts came to me.) But it was another instance of his weakness and lassitude.

"My theory is that he has probably gone to South America, or thrown himself off a bridge—because he saw that there was no future for him if he were always to take pictures of shells and things. And he was weak. The weak can never face themselves, and so cannot see the practical side of the world, how things are laid out, and what sacrifices are required to survive and prosper. It is only in fairy tales that they rise to triumph."

Wallich could not afford to get to South America. He certainly would not have thrown himself off a bridge. He was excessively neat and orderly, and the prospect of some poor fireman handling a swollen, bloated body resounding with flies deterred him forever from such nonsense.

Perhaps if he had been a Gypsy he would have taken to the road. But he was no Gypsy, and had not the talent, skill, or taste for life outside Bavaria. Only once had he been away, to Paris. It was their honeymoon, when he and his wife did not need Paris or any city. They went by train and stayed for a week at a hotel by the Quai Voltaire. They walked in the gardens all day long, and in the May evenings they went to concerts where they heard the perfect music of their own country. Though they were away for just a week, and read the German papers, and went to a corner of the Luxembourg Gardens where there were pines and wildflowers like those in the greenbelt around Munich, this music made them sick for home. They re-turned two days early and never left again except for July and August, which each year they spent in the Black For-est, at a cabin inherited from her parents.

He dared not go back to that cabin. It was set like a trap. Were he to enter he would be enfiladed by the sight of their son's pictures and toys, his little boots and minia-ture fishing rod, and by her comb lying at the exact angle she had left it when she had last brushed her hair, and by the sweet smell of her clothing. No, someday he would have to burn the cabin. He dared not sell, for strangers then would handle roughly all those things which meant so much to him that he could not even gaze upon them. He left the little cabin to stand empty, perhaps the object of an occasional hiker's curiosity, or recipient of cheerful postcards from friends traveling or at the beach for the summer—friends who had not heard.

He sought instead a town far enough from Munich so that he would not encounter anything familiar, a place where he would be unrecognized and yet a place not entirely strange, where he would have to undergo no savage adjustments, where he could buy a Munich paper.

A search of the map brought his flying eye always southward to the borderlands, to Alpine country remarkable for the steepness of the brown contours, the depth of the valleys, and the paucity of settled places. Those few depicted towns appeared to be clean and well placed on high overlooks. Unlike the cities to the north—circles which clustered together on the flatlands or along rivers, like colonies of bacteria—the cities of the Alps stood alone, *in extremis,* near the border. Though he dared not cross the border, he thought perhaps to venture near its edge, to see what he would see. These isolated towns in the Alps promised shining clear air and deep-green trees. Perhaps they were above the tree line. In a number of cases it looked that way—and the circles were far from resembling clusters of bacteria. They seemed like untethered balloons.

He chose a town for its ridiculous name, reasoning that few of his friends would desire to travel to such a place. The world bypasses badly named towns as easily as it abandons ungainly children. It was called Garmisch-Partenkirchen. At the station in Munich, they did not even inscribe the full name on his ticket, writing merely "Garmisch-P."

"Do you live there?" the railroad agent had asked.

"No," answered Wallich.

"Are you visiting relatives, or going on business, or going to ski?"

"No."

"Then perhaps you are making a mistake. To go in October is not wise, if you do not ski. As unbelievable as it may seem, they have had much snow. Why go now?"

"I am a mountain climber," answered Wallich.

"In winter?" The railway agent was used to flushing out lies, and when little fat Austrian boys just old enough for adult tickets would bend their knees at his window as if at confession and say in squeaky voices, "Half fare to Salzburg!," he pounced upon them as if he were a leopard and they juicy ptarmigan or baby roebuck.

"Yes, in the winter," Wallich said. "Good mountain climbers thrive in difficult conditions. The more ice, the more storm, the greater the accomplishment. I am accumulating various winter records. In January, I go to America, where I will ascend their highest mountain, Mt. Independence, four thousand meters." He blushed so hard that the railway agent followed suit. Then Wallich backed away, insensibly mortified.

A mountain climber! He would close his eyes in fear when looking through Swiss calendars. He had not the stamina to rush up the stairs to his studio. He had failed miserably at sports. He was not a mountain climber, and had never even dreamed of being one.

Yet when his train pulled out of the vault of lacy ironwork and late-afternoon shadow, its steam exhalations were like those of a man puffing up a high meadow, speeding to reach the rock and ice, and Wallich felt as if he were embarking upon an ordeal of the type men experience on the precipitous rock walls of great cloud-swirled peaks. Why was he going to Garmisch-Partenkirchen anyway, if not for an ordeal through which to right himself? He was pulled so far over on one side by the death of his family, he was so bent and crippled by the pain of it, that he was going to Garmisch-Partenkirchen to suffer a parallel ordeal through which he would balance what had befallen him.

How wrong his parents and friends had been when

they had offered help as his business faltered. A sensible, graceful man will have symmetry. He remembered the time at youth camp when a stream had changed course away from a once gushing sluice and the younger boys had had to carry buckets of water up a small hill, to fill a cistern. The skinny little boys had struggled up the hill. Their counselor, sitting comfortably in the shade, would not let them go two to a bucket. At first they had tried to carry the pails in front of them, but this was nearly impossible. Then they surreptitiously spilled half the water on the way up, until the counselor took up position at the cistern and inspected each cargo. It had been torture to carry the heavy bucket in one aching hand. Wallich finally decided to take two buckets. Though it was agony, it was a better agony than the one he had had, because he had retrieved his balance, could look ahead, and, by carrying a double burden, had strengthened himself and made the job that much shorter. Soon, all the boys carried two buckets. The cistern was filled in no time, and they had a victory over their surprised counselor.

So, he thought as the train shuttled through chill half-harvested fields, I will be a hermit in Garmisch-Partenkirchen. I will know no one. I will be alone. I may even begin to climb mountains. Perhaps I will lose fingers and toes, and on the way gather a set of wounds which will allow me some peace.

He sensed the change of landscape before he actually came upon it. Then they began to climb, and the engine sweated steam from steel to carry the lumbering cars up terrifying grades on either side of which blue pines stood angled against the mountainside. They reached a level stretch which made the train curve like a dragon and led it through deep tunnels, and they sped along as if on a summer excursion, with views of valleys so distant that in them whole forests sat upon their meadows like birth-marks, and streams were little more than the grain in leather.

Wallich opened his window and leaned out, watching ahead for tunnels. The air was thick and cold. It was full of sunshine and greenery, and it flowed past as if it were a mountain river. When he pulled back, his cheeks were red and his face pounded from the frigid air. He was alone in the compartment. By the time the lights came on he had decided upon the course of an ideal. He was to become a mountain climber, after all—and in a singularly difficult, dangerous, and satisfying way.

A porter said in passing the compartment, "The dining car is open, sir." Service to the Alps was famed. Even though his journey was no more than two hours, he had arranged to eat on the train, and had paid for and ordered a meal to which he looked forward in pleasant anticipation, especially because he had selected French strawberries in cream for dessert. But then he saw his body in the gently lit half mirror. He was soft from a lifetime of near-happiness. The sight of his face in the blond light of the mirror made him decide to begin preparing for the mountains that very evening. The porter ate the strawberries.

Of the many ways to attempt an ordeal perhaps the most graceful and attractive is the Alpine. It is far more satisfying than Oriental starvation and abnegation precisely because the European ideal is to commit difficult acts amid richness and overflowing beauty. For that reason, the Alpine is as well the most demanding. It is hard to deny oneself, to pare oneself down, at the heart and base of a civilization so full.

Wallich rode to Garmisch-Partenkirchen in a thunder of proud Alps. The trees were tall and lively, the air crystalline, and radiating beams spoke through the train window from one glowing range to another. A world of high ice laughed. And yet ranks of competing images assaulted him. He had gasped at the sight of Bremen, a port stuffed with iron ships gushing wheat steam from their whistles as they prepared to sail. In the mountain dryness, he remembered humid ports from which these massive ships crossed a colorful world, bringing back on laden decks a catalogue of stuffs and curiosities.

Golden images of the north plains struck from the left. The salt-white plains nearly floated above the sea. All this was in Germany, though Germany was just a small part of the world, removed almost entirely from the deep source of things—from the high lakes where explorers touched the silvers which caught the world's images, from the Sahara where they found the fine glass which bent the light.

Arriving at Garmisch-Partenkirchen in the dark, he could hear bells chiming and water rushing. Cool currents of air flowed from the direction of this white tumbling sound. It was winter. He hailed a horse-drawn sledge and piled his baggage in the back. "Hotel Aufburg," he said authoritatively.

"Hotel Aufburg?" asked the driver.

"Yes, Hotel Aufburg. There is such a place, isn't there? It hasn't closed, has it?"

"No, sir, it hasn't closed." The driver touched his horse with the whip. The horse walked twenty feet and was reined to a stop. "Here we are," the driver said. "I trust you've had a pleasant journey. Time passes quickly up here in the mountains."

The sign for the hotel was so large and well lit that the street in front of it shone as in daylight. The driver was guffawing to himself; the little guffaws rumbled about in him like subterranean thunder. He could not wait to tell the other drivers.

Wallich did nothing properly in Garmisch-Partenkirchen. But it was a piece of luck that he felt too awkward and ill at ease to sit alone in restaurants while, nearby, families and lovers had self-centered raucous meals, sometimes even bursting into song. Winter took over the town and covered it in stiff white ice. The unresilient cold, the troikas jingling through the streets, the frequent snowfalls encouraged winter fat. But because Wallich ate cold food in his room or stopped occasionally at a counter for a steaming bowl of soup, he became a shadow.

The starvation was pleasant. It made him sleepy and its constant physical presence gave him companionship. He sat for hours watching the snow, feeling as if he were part of it, as if the diminution of his body were great progress, as if such lightening would lessen his sorrow and bring him to the high rim of things he had not seen before, things which would help him and show him what to do and make him proud just for coming upon them.

He began to exercise. Several times a day the hotel manager knocked like a woodpecker at Wallich's door. The angrier the manager, the faster the knocks. If he were really angry, he spoke so rapidly that he sounded like a speeded-up record: "Herr Wallich, I must ask you on behalf of the other guests to stop immediately all the thumping and vibration! This is a quiet hotel, in a quiet town, in a quiet tourist region. Please!" Then the manager would bow and quickly withdraw.

Eventually they threw Wallich out, but not before he had spent October and November in concentrated maniacal pursuit of physical strength. He had started with five each, every waking hour, of pushups, pull-ups, sit-ups, toe-touches, and leg-raises. The pull-ups were deadly—he did one every twelve minutes. The thumping and bumping came from five minutes of running in place. At the end of the first day, the pain in his chest was so intense that he was certain he was not long for the world. The second day was worse. And so it went, until after ten days there was no pain at all. The weight he abandoned helped a great deal to expand his physical prowess. He was, after all, in his middle twenties, and had never eaten to excess. Nor did he smoke or drink, except for champagne at weddings and municipal celebrations. In fact, he had always had rather ascetic tendencies, and had thought it fitting to have spent his life in Munich—"Home of Monks."

By his fifteenth day in Garmisch-Partenkirchen he had increased his schedule to fifteen apiece of the exercises each hour, which meant, for example, that he did a pull-up every four minutes whenever he was awake. Late at night he ran aimlessly about the deserted streets for an hour or more, even though it sometimes snowed. Two policemen who huddled over a brazier in their tiny booth simply looked at one another and pointed to their heads, twirling their fingers and rolling their eyes every time he passed by. On the last day of November, he moved up the valley to a little village called Altenburg-St. Peter.

There it was worse in some ways and better in others. Altenburg-St. Peter was so tiny that no stranger could enter unobserved, and so still that no one could do anything without the knowledge of the entire community. Children stared at Wallich on the street. This made him walk on the little lanes and approach his few destinations from the rear, which led housewives to speculate that he was a burglar. There were few merchants, and, because they were cousins, they could with little effort determine exactly what Wallich ate. When one week they were positive that he had consumed only four bowls of soup, a pound of cheese, a pound of smoked meat, a quart of yogurt, and two loaves of bread, they were incredulous. They themselves ate this much in a day. They wondered how Wallich survived on so little. Finally they came up with an answer. He received packages from Munich several times a week and in these packages was food, they thought—and probably very great delicacies. Then as the winter got harder and the snows covered everything they stopped wondering about him. They did not see him as he ran out of his lodgings at midnight, and the snow muffled his tread. He ran up the road toward the Schreuderspitze, first for a kilometer, then two, then five, then ten, then twenty—when finally he had to stop because he had begun slipping in just before the farmers arose and would have seen him.

By the end of February the packages had ceased arriving, and he was a changed man. No one would have mistaken him for what he had been. In five months he had become lean and strong. He did two hundred and fifty sequential pushups at least four times a day. For the sheer pleasure of it, he would do a hundred and fifty pushups on his fingertips. Every day he did a hundred pull-ups in a row. His midnight run, sometimes in snow which had accumulated up to his knees, was four hours long.

The packages had contained only books on climbing, and equipment. At first the books had been terribly discouraging. Every elementary text had bold warnings in red or green ink: "It is extremely dangerous to attempt genuine ascents without proper training. This volume should be used in conjunction with a certified course on climbing, or with the advice of a registered guide. A book itself will not do!"

One manual had in bright-red ink, on the very last page: "Go back, you fool! Certain death awaits you!" Wallich imagined that, as the books said, there were many things he could not learn except by human example, and many mistakes he might make in interpreting the manuals, which would go uncorrected save for the critique of living practitioners. But it didn't matter. He was determined to learn for himself and accomplish his task alone. Besides, since the accident he had become a recluse, and could hardly speak. The thought of enrolling in a climbing school full of young people from all parts of the country paralyzed him. How could he reconcile his task with their enthusiasm? For them it was recreation, perhaps something aesthetic or spiritual, a way to meet new friends. For him it was one tight channel through which he would either burst on to a new life, or in which he would die.

Studying carefully, he soon worked his way to advanced treaties for those who had spent years in the Alps. He understood these well enough, having quickly learned the terminologies and the humor and the faults of those who write about the mountains. He was even convinced that he knew the spirit in which the treatises had been written, for though he had never climbed, he had only to look out his window to see high white mountains about which blue sky swirled like a banner. He felt that in seeing them he was one of them, and was greatly encouraged when he read in a French mountaineer's memoirs: "After years in the mountains, I learned to look upon a given range and feel as if I were the last peak in the line. Thus I felt the music of the empty spaces enwrapping me, and I became not an intruder on the cliffs, dangling only to drop away, but an equal in transit. I seldom looked at my own body but only at the mountains, and my eyes felt like the eyes of the mountains."

He lavished nearly all his dwindling money on fine equipment. He calculated that after his purchases he would have enough to live on through September. Then he would have nothing. He had expended large sums on the best tools, and he spent the intervals between his hours of reading and exercise holding and studying the shiny carabiners, pitons, slings, chocks, hammers, ice pitons, axes, étriers, crampons, ropes, and specialized hardware that he had either ordered or constructed himself from plans in the advanced books.

It was insane, he knew, to funnel all his preparation into a few months of agony and then without any experience whatever throw himself alone onto a Class VI ascent—the seldom climbed *Westgebirgsausläufer* of the Schreuderspitze. Not having driven one piton, he was going to attempt a five-day climb up the nearly sheer western counterfort. Even in late June, he would spend a third of his time on ice. But the sight of the ice in March, shining like a faraway sword over the cold and absolute distance, drove him on. He had long passed censure. Had anyone known what he was doing and tried to dissuade him, he would have told him to go to hell, and resumed preparations with the confidence of someone taken up by a new religion.

For he had always believed in great deeds, in fairy tales, in echoing trumpet lands, in wonders and wondrous accomplishments. But even as a boy he had never considered that such things would fall to him. As a good city child he had known that these adventures were not necessary. But suddenly he was alone and the things which occurred to him were great warlike deeds. His energy and discipline were boundless, as full and overflowing as a lake in the mountains. Like the heroes of his youth, he would try to approach the high cord of ruby light and bend it to his will, until he could feel rolling thunder. The small things, the gentle things, the good things he loved, and the flow of love itself were dead for him and would always be, unless he could liberate them in a crucible of high drama.

It took him many months to think these things, and though they might not seem consistent, they were so for him, and he often spent hours alone on a sunny snow-covered meadow, his elbows on his knees, imagining great deeds in the mountains, as he stared at the massive needle of the Schreuderspitze, at the hint of rich lands beyond, and at the tiny village where he had taken up position opposite the mountain.

Toward the end of May he had been walking through Altenburg-St. Peter and seen his reflection in a store window—a storm had arisen suddenly and made the glass as silver-black as the clouds. He had not liked what he had seen. His face had become too hard and too lean. There was not enough gentleness. He feared immediately for the success of his venture if only because he knew well that unmitigated extremes are a great cause of failure. And he was tired of his painful regimen.

He bought a large Telefunken radio, in one fell swoop wiping out his funds for August and September. He felt as if he were paying for the privilege of music with portions of his life and body. But it was well worth it. When the storekeeper offered to deliver the heavy console, Wallich declined politely, picked up the cabinet himself, hoisted it on his back, and walked out of the store bent under it as in classic illustrations for physics textbooks throughout the industrialized world. He did not put it down once. The storekeeper summoned his associates and they bet and counterbet on whether Wallich "would" or "would not," as he moved slowly up the steep hill, up the steps, around the white switchbacks, onto a grassy slope, and then finally up the precipitous stairs to the balcony outside his room. "How can he have done that?" they asked. "He is a small man, and the radio must weigh at least thirty kilos." The storekeeper trotted out with a catalogue. "It weighs fifty-five kilograms!" he said. "Fifty-five kilograms!" And they wondered what had made Wallich so strong.

Once, Wallich had taken his little son (a tiny, skeptical, silent child who had a riotous giggle which could last for an hour) to see the inflation of a great gas dirigible. It had been a disappointment, for a dirigible is rigid and maintains always the same shape. He had expected to see the silver of its sides expand into ribbed cliffs which would float over them on the green field and amaze his son. Now that silver rising, the sail-like expansion, the great crescendo of a glimmering weightless mass, finally reached him alone in his room, too late but well received, when a Berlin station played the Beethoven Violin Concerto, its first five timpanic D's like grace before a feast. After those notes, the music lifted him, and he riveted his gaze on the dark shapes of the mountains, where a lightning storm raged. The radio crackled after each near or distant flash, but it was as if the music had been designed for it. Wallich looked at the yellow light within a softly glowing numbered panel. It flickered gently, and he could hear cracks and flashes in the music as he saw them delineated across darkness. They looked and sounded like the bent riverine limbs of dead trees hanging majestically over rocky outcrops, destined to fall, but enjoying their grand suspension nonetheless. The music traveled effortlessly on anarchic beams, passed high over the plains, passed high the forests, seeding them plentifully, and came upon the Alps like waves which finally strike the shore after thousands of miles in open sea. It charged upward, mating with the electric storm, separating, and delivering.

To Wallich—alone in the mountains, surviving amid the dark massifs and clear air—came the closeted, nasal, cosmopolitan voice of the radio commentator. It was good to know that there was something other than the purity and magnificence of his mountains, that far to the north the balance reverted to less than moral catastrophe and death, and much stock was set in things of extraordinary inconsequence. Wallich could not help laughing when he thought of the formally dressed audience at the symphony, how they squirmed in their seats and heated the bottoms of their trousers and capes, how relieved and delighted they would be to step out into the cool evening and go to a restaurant. In the morning they would arise and take pleasure from the sweep of the drapes as sun danced by, from the gold rim around a white china cup. For them it was always too hot or too cold. But they certainly had their delights, about which sometimes he would think. How often he still dreamed, asleep or awake, of the smooth color plates opulating under his hands in tanks of developer and of the fresh film which smelled like bread and then was entombed in black cylinders to develop. How he longed sometimes for the precise machinery of his cameras. The very word *"Kamera"* was as dark and hollow as this night in the mountains when, reviewing the pleasures of faraway Berlin, he sat in perfect health and equanimity upon a wickerweave seat in a bare white room. The only light was from the yellow dial, the sudden lightning flashes, and the faint blue of the sky beyond the hills. And all was quiet but for the music and the thunder and the static

curling about the music like weak and lost memories
which arise to harry even indomitable perfections.

A month before the ascent, he awaited arrival of a good
climbing rope. He needed from a rope not strength to hold
a fall but lightness and length for abseiling. His strategy
was to climb with a short self-belay. No one would follow
to retrieve his hardware and because it would not always
be practical for him to do so himself, in what one of his
books called "rhythmic recapitulation," he planned to
carry a great deal of metal. If the metal and he reached
the summit relatively intact, he could make short work
of the descent, abandoning pitons as he abseiled downward.

He would descend in half a day that which had taken
five days to climb. He pictured the abseiling, literally a
flight down the mountain on the doubled cord of his long
rope, and he thought that those hours speeding down the
cliffs would be the finest of his life. If the weather were
good he would come away from the Schreuderspitze having flown like an eagle.

On the day the rope was due, he went to the railroad
station to meet the mail. It was a clear, perfect day. The
light was so fine and rich that in its bath everyone felt wise,
strong, and content. Wallich sat on the wooden boards of
the wide platform, scanning the green meadows and fields
for smoke and a coal engine, but the countryside was silent
and the valley unmarred by the black woolly chain he
sought. In the distance, toward France and Switzerland,
a few cream-and-rose-colored clouds rode the horizon, im-
mobile and high. On far mountainsides innumerable flowers showed in this long view as a slash, or as a patch of
color not unlike one flower alone.

He had arrived early, for he had no watch. After

some minutes a car drove up and from it emerged a young family. They rushed as if the train were waiting to depart, when down the long troughlike valley it was not even visible. There were two little girls, as beautiful as he had ever seen. The mother, too, was extraordinarily fine. The father was in his early thirties, and he wore gold-rimmed glasses. They seemed like a university family—people who knew how to live sensibly, taking pleasure from proper and beautiful things.

The littler girl was no more than three. Sunburnt and rosy, she wore a dress that was shaped like a bell. She dashed about the platform so lightly and tentatively that it was as if Wallich were watching a tiny fish gravityless in a lighted aquarium. Her older sister stood quietly by the mother, who was illumined with consideration and pride for her children. It was apparent that she was overjoyed with the grace of her family. She seemed detached and preoccupied, but in just the right way. The littler girl said in a voice like a child's party horn, "Mummy, I want some peanuts!"

It was so ridiculous that this child should share the appetite of elephants that the mother smiled. "Peanuts will make you thirsty, Gretl. Wait until we get to Garmisch-Partenkirchen. Then we'll have lunch in the buffet."

"When will we get to Garmisch-Partenkirchen?"

"At two."

"Two?"

"Yes, at two."

"At two?"

"Gretl!"

The father looked alternately at the mountains and at his wife and children. He seemed confident and stead-

fast. In the distance black smoke appeared in thick billows. The father pointed at it. "There's our train," he said.

"Where?" asked Gretl, looking in the wrong direction. The father picked her up and turned her head with
his hand, aiming her gaze down the shimmering valley.
When she saw the train she started, and her eyes opened
wide in pleasure.

"Ah . . . there it is," said the father. As the train
pulled into the station the young girls were filled with excitement. Amid the noise they entered a compartment and
were swallowed up in the steam. The train pulled out.

Wallich stood on the empty platform, unwrapping
his rope. It was a rope, quite a nice rope, but it did not
make him as happy as he had expected it would.

Little can match the silhouette of mountains by night. The
great mass becomes far more mysterious when its face is
darkened, when its sweeping lines roll steeply into valleys
and peaks and long impossible ridges, when behind the
void a concoction of rare silver leaps up to trace the
hills—the pressure of collected starlight. That night, in
conjunction with the long draughts of music he had become used to taking, he began to dream his dreams. They
did not frighten him—he was beyond fear, too strong for
fear, too played out. They did not even puzzle him, for
they unfolded like the chapters in a brilliant nine-
teenth-century history. The rich explanations filled him
for days afterward. He was amazed, and did not understand why these perfect dreams suddenly came to him.
Surely they did not arise from within. He had never had
the world so beautifully portrayed, had never seen as
clearly and in such sure, gentle steps, had never risen so
high and so smoothly in unfolding enlightenment, and he
had seldom felt so well looked after. And yet, there was

no visible presence. But it was as if the mountains and valleys were filled with loving families of which he was part.

Upon his return from the railroad platform, a storm had come suddenly from beyond the southern ridge. Though it had been warm and clear that day, he had seen from the sunny meadow before his house that a white storm billowed in higher and higher curves, pushing itself over the summits, finally to fall like an air avalanche on the valley. It snowed on the heights. The sun continued to strike the opaque frost and high clouds. It did not snow in the valley. The shock troops of the storm remained at the highest elevations, and only worn gray veterans came below—misty clouds and rain on cold wet air. Ragged clouds moved across the mountainsides and meadows, watering the trees and sometimes catching in low places. Even so, the air in the meadow was still horn-clear.

In his room that night Wallich rocked back and forth on the wicker chair (it was not a rocker and he knew that using it as such was to number its days). That night's crackling infusion from Berlin, rising warmly from the faintly lit dial, was Beethoven's Eighth. The familiar commentator, nicknamed by Wallich Mälzels Metronom because of his even monotone, discoursed upon the background of the work.

"For many years," he said, "no one except Beethoven liked this symphony. Beethoven's opinions, however—even regarding his own creations—are equal at least to the collective pronouncements of all the musicologists and critics alive in the West during any hundred-year period. Conscious of the merits of the F-Major Symphony, he resolutely determined to redeem and . . . ah . . . the conductor has arrived. He steps to the podium. We begin."

Wallich retired that night in perfect tranquillity but awoke at five in the morning soaked in his own sweat, his fists clenched, a terrible pain in his chest, and breathing heavily as if he had been running. In the dim unattended light of the early-morning storm, he lay with eyes wide open. His pulse subsided, but he was like an animal in a cave, like a creature who has just escaped an organized hunt. It was as if the whole village had come armed and in search of him, had by some miracle decided that he was not in, and had left to comb the wet woods. He had been dreaming, and he saw his dream in its exact form. It was, first, an emerald. Cut into an octagon with two long sides, it was shaped rather like the plaque at the bottom of a painting. Events within this emerald were circular and never-ending.

They were in Munich. Air and sun were refined as on the station platform in the mountains. He was standing at a streetcar stop with his wife and his two daughters, though he knew perfectly well in the dream that these two daughters were meant to be his son. A streetcar arrived in complete silence. Clouds of people began to embark. They were dressed and muffled in heavy clothing of dull blue and gray. To his surprise, his wife moved toward the door of the streetcar and started to board, the daughters trailing after her. He could not see her feet, and she moved in a glide. Though at first paralyzed, as in the instant before a crash, he did manage to bound after her. As she stepped onto the first step and was about to grasp a chrome pole within the doorway, he made for her arm and caught it.

He pulled her back and spun her around, all very gently. Her presence before him was so intense that it was as if he were trapped under the weight of a fallen beam. She, too, wore a winter coat, but it was slim and perfectly tailored. He remembered the perfect geometry of the lapels. Not on earth had such angles ever been seen. The

coat was a most intense liquid emerald color, a living
light-infused green. She had always looked best in green,
for her hair was like shining gold. He stood before her.
He felt her delicacy. Her expression was neutral. "Where
are you going?" he asked incredulously.

"I must go," she said.

He put his arms around her. She returned his em-
brace, and he said, "How can you leave me?"

"I have to," she answered.

And then she stepped onto the first step of the streetcar, and onto the second step, and she was enfolded into
darkness.

He awoke, feeling like an invalid. His strength served
for naught. He just stared at the clouds lifting higher and
higher as the storm cleared. By nightfall the sky was black
and gentle, though very cold. He kept thinking back to
the emerald. It meant everything to him, for it was the
first time he realized that they were really dead. Silence
followed. Time passed thickly. He could not have imagined the sequence of dreams to follow, and what they
would do to him.

He began to fear sleep, thinking that he would again be
subjected to the lucidity of the emerald. But he had run
that course and would never do so again except by perfect
conscious recollection. The night after he had the dream
of the emerald he fell asleep like someone letting go of a
cliff edge after many minutes alone without help or hope.
He slid into sleep, heart beating wildly. To his surprise,
he found himself far indeed from the trolley tracks in Munich.

Instead, he was alone in the center of a sunlit snow-
field, walking on the glacier in late June, bound for the
summit of the Schreuderspitze. The mass of his equipment

sat lightly upon him. He was well drilled in its use and positioning, in the subtleties of placement and rigging. The things he carried seemed part of him, as if he had quickly evolved into a new kind of animal suited for breathtaking travel in the steep heights.

His stride was light and long, like that of a man on the moon. He nearly floated, ever so slightly airborne, over the dazzling glacier. He leaped crevasses, sailing in slow motion against intense white and blue. He passed apple-fresh streams and opalescent melt pools of blue-green water as he progressed toward the Schreuder-spitze. Its rocky horn was covered by nearly blue ice from which the wind blew a white corona in sines and cusps twirling about the sky.

Passing the bergschrund, he arrived at the first mass of rock. He turned to look back. There he saw the snow-field and the sun turning above it like a pinwheel, casting out a fog of golden light. He stood alone. The world had been reduced to the beauty of physics and the mystery of light. It had been rendered into a frozen state, a liquid state, a solid state, a gaseous state, mixtures, temperatures, and more varieties of light than fell on the speckled floor of a great cathedral. It was simple, and yet infinitely complex. The sun was warm. There was silence.

For several hours he climbed over great boulders and up a range of rocky escarpments. It grew more and more difficult, and he often had to lay in protection, driving a piton into a crack of the firm granite. His first piton was a surprise. It slowed halfway, and the ringing sound as he hammered grew higher in pitch. Finally, it would go in no farther. He had spent so much time in driving it that he thought it would be as steady as the Bank of England. But when he gave a gentle tug to test its hold, it came right out. This he thought extremely funny. He then remembered that he had either to drive it in all the way, to the eye, or to attach a sling along its shaft as near as possible to the rock. It was a question of avoiding leverage.

He bent carefully to his equipment sling, replaced the used piton, and took up a shorter one. The shorter piton went to its eye in five hammer strokes and he could do nothing to dislodge it. He clipped in and ascended a steep pitch, at the top of which he drove in two pitons, tied in to them, abseiled down to retrieve the first, and ascended quite easily to where he had left off. He made rapid progress over frightening pitches, places no one would dare go without assurance of a bolt in the rock and a line to the bolt—even if the bolt was just a small piece of metal driven in by dint of precariously balanced strength, arm, and Alpine hammer.

Within the sphere of utter concentration easily achieved during difficult ascents, his simple climbing evolved naturally into graceful technique, by which he went up completely vertical rock faces, suspended only by pitons and étriers. The different placements of which he had read and thought repeatedly were employed skillfully and with a proper sense of variety, though it was tempting to stay with one familiar pattern. Pounding metal into rock and hanging from his taut and colorful wires, he breathed hard, he concentrated, and he went up sheer walls.

At one point he came to the end of a subtle hairline crack in an otherwise smooth wall. The rock above was completely solid for a hundred feet. If he went down to the base of the crack he would be nowhere. The only thing to do was to make a swing traverse to a wall more amenable to climbing.

Anchoring two pitons into the rock as solidly as he could, he clipped an oval carabiner on the bottom piton,

put a safety line on the top one, and lowered himself about
sixty feet down the two ropes. Hanging perpendicular to
the wall, he began to walk back and forth across the rock.
He moved to and fro, faster and faster, until he was running. Finally he touched only in places and was swinging
wildly like a pendulum. He feared that the piton to which
he was anchored would not take the strain, and would pull
out. But he kept swinging faster, until he gave one final
push and, with a pathetic cry, went sailing over a drop
which would have made a mountain goat swallow its
heart. He caught an outcropping of rock on the other side,
and pulled himself to it desperately. He hammered in, retrieved the ropes, glanced at the impassable wall, and
began again to ascend.

As he approached great barricades of ice, he looked
back. It gave him great pride and satisfaction to see the
thousands of feet over which he had struggled. Much of
the west counterfort was purely vertical. He could see now
just how the glacier was riverine. He could see deep within
the Tyrol and over the border to the Swiss lakes. Garmisch-Partenkirchen looked from here like a town
on the board of a toy railroad or (if considered only
two-dimensionally) like the cross-section of a kidney. Altenburg-St. Peter looked like a ladybug. The sun sent
streamers of tan light through the valley, already
three-quarters conquered by shadow, and the ice above
took fire. Where the ice began, he came to a wide ledge
and he stared upward at a sparkling ridge which looked
like a great crystal spine. Inside, it was blue and cold.

He awoke, convinced that he had in fact climbed the
counterfort. It was a strong feeling, as strong as the reality
of the emerald. Sometimes dreams could be so real that
they competed with the world, riding at even balance and
calling for a decision. Sometimes, he imagined, when they

are so real and so important, they easily tip the scale and
the world buckles and dreams become real. Crossing the
fragile barricades, one enters his dreams, thinking of his
life as imagined.

He rejoiced at his bravery in climbing. It had been
as real as anything he had ever experienced. He felt the
pain, the exhaustion, and the reward, as well as the danger. But he could not wait to return to the mountain and
the ice. He longed for evening and the enveloping darkness, believing that he belonged resting under great folds
of ice on the wall of the Schreuderspitze. He had no patience with his wicker chair, the bent wood of the window-
sill, the clear glass in the window, the green-sided hills he
saw curving through it, or his brightly colored equipment
hanging from pegs on the white wall.

Two weeks before, on one of the eastward roads from Altenburg-St. Peter—no more than a dirt track—he had
seen a child turn and take a well-worn path toward a
wood, a meadow, and a stream by which stood a house
and a barn. The child walked slowly upward into the forest, disappearing into the dark close, as if he had been
taken up by vapor. Wallich had been too far away to hear
footsteps, and the last thing he saw was the back of the
boy's bright blue-and-white sweater. Returning at dusk,
Wallich had expected to see warmly lit windows, and
smoke issuing efficiently from the straight chimney. But
there were no lights, and there was no smoke. He made
his way through the trees and past the meadow only to
come upon a small farmhouse with boarded windows and
no-trespassing signs tacked on the doors.

It was unsettling when he saw the same child making
his way across the upper meadow, a flash of blue and white
in the near darkness. Wallich screamed out to him, but

he did not hear, and kept walking as if he were deaf or in another world, and he went over the crest of the hill. Wallich ran up the hill. When he reached the top he saw only a wide empty field and not a trace of the boy.

Then in the darkness and purity of the meadows he began to feel that the world had many secrets, that they were shattering even to glimpse or sense, and that they were not necessarily unpleasant. In certain states of light he could see, he could begin to sense, things most miraculous indeed. Although it seemed self-serving, he concluded nonetheless, after a lifetime of adhering to the diffuse principles of a science he did not know, that there was life after death, that the dead rose into a mischievous world of pure light, that something most mysterious lay beyond the enfolding darkness, something wonderful.

This idea had taken hold, and he refined it. For example, listening to the Beethoven symphonies broadcast from Berlin, he began to think that they were like a ladder of mountains, that they surpassed themselves and rose higher and higher until at certain points they seemed to break the warp itself and cross into a heaven of light and the dead. There were signs everywhere of temporal diffusion and mystery. It was as if continents existed, new worlds lying just off the coast, invisible and redolent, waiting for the grasp of one man suddenly to substantiate and light them, changing everything. Perhaps great mountains hundreds of times higher than the Alps would arise in the sea or on the flatlands. They might be purple or gold and shining in many states of refraction and reflection, transparent in places as vast as countries. Someday someone would come back from this place, or someone would by accident discover and illumine its remarkable physics.

He believed that the boy he had seen nearly glowing in the half-darkness of the high meadow had been his son,

and that the child had been teasing his father in a way only
he could know, that the child had been asking him to follow. Possibly he had come upon great secrets on the other
side, and knew that his father would join him soon enough
and that then they would laugh about the world.

When he next fell asleep in the silence of a clear wind-
less night in the valley, Wallich was like a man disappearing into the warp of darkness. He wanted to go there, to
be taken as far as he could be taken. He was not unlike
a sailor who sets sail in the teeth of a great storm, delighted by his own abandon.

Throwing off the last wraps of impure light, he found
himself again in the ice world. The word was
all-encompassing—*Eiswelt*. There above him the blue
spire rocketed upward as far as the eye could see. He
touched it with his hand. It was indeed as cold as ice. It
was dense and hard, like glass ten feet thick. He had
doubted its strength, but its solidity told that it would not
flake away and allow him to drop endlessly, far from it.

On ice he found firm holds both with his feet and with
his hands, and hardly needed the ice pitons and étriers.
For he had crampons tied firmly to his boots, and could
spike his toe points into the ice and stand comfortably on
a vertical. He proceeded with a surety of footing he had
never had on the streets of Munich. Each step bolted him
down to the surface. And in each hand he carried an ice
hammer with which he made swinging, cutting arcs that
engaged the shining stainless-steel pick with the mirror-
like wall.

All the snow had blown away or had melted. There
were no traps, no pitfalls, no ambiguities. He progressed
toward the summit rapidly, climbing steep ice walls as if
he had been going up a ladder. The air became purer and
the light more direct. Looking out to right or left, or glanc-

ing sometimes over his shoulders, he saw that he was now truly in the world of mountains.

Above the few clouds he could see only equal peaks of ice, and the Schreuderspitze dropping away from him. It was not the world of rock. No longer could he make out individual features in the valley. Green had become a hazy dark blue appropriate to an ocean floor. Whole countries came into view. The landscape was a mass of winding glaciers and great mountains. At that height, all was separated and refined. Soft things vanished, and there remained only the white and the silver.

He did not reach the summit until dark. He did not see the stars because icy clouds covered the Schreuder-spitze in a crystalline fog which flowed past, crackling and hissing. He was heartbroken to have come all the way to the summit and then be blinded by masses of clouds. Since he could not descend until light, he decided to stay firmly stationed until he could see clearly. Meanwhile, he lost patience and began to address a presence in the air—casually, not thinking it strange to do so, not thinking twice about talking to the void.

He awoke in his room in early morning, saying, "All these blinding clouds. Why all these blinding clouds?"

Though the air of the valley was as fresh as a flower, he detested it. He pulled the covers over his head and strove for unconsciousness, but he grew too hot and finally gave up, staring at the remnants of dawn light soaking about his room. The day brightened in the way that stage lights come up, suddenly brilliant upon a beam-washed platform. It was early June. He had lost track of the exact date, but he knew that sometime before he had crossed into June. He had lost them early in June. Two years had passed.

He packed his things. Though he had lived like a monk, much had accumulated, and this he put into suitcases, boxes, and bags. He packed his pens, paper, books, a chess set on which he sometimes played against an imaginary opponent named Herr Claub, the beautiful Swiss calendars upon which he had at one time been almost afraid to gaze, cooking equipment no more complex than a soldier's mess kit, his clothing, even the beautifully wrought climbing equipment, for, after all, he had another set, up there in the *Eiswelt*. Only his bedding remained unpacked. It was on the floor in the center of the room, where he slept. He put some banknotes in an envelope—the June rent—and tacked it to the doorpost. The room was empty, white, and it would have echoed had it been slightly larger. He would say something and then listen intently, his eyes flaring like those of a lunatic. He had not eaten in days, and was not disappointed that even the waking world began to seem like a dream.

He went to the pump. He had accustomed himself to bathing in streams so cold that they were too frightened to freeze. Clean and cleanly shaven, he returned to his room. He smelled the sweet pine scent he had brought back on his clothing after hundreds of trips through the woods and forests girdling the greater mountains. Even the bedding was snowy white. He opened the closet and caught a glimpse of himself in the mirror. He was dark from sun and wind; his hair shone; his face had thinned; his eyebrows were now gold and white. For several days he had had only cold pure water. Like soldiers who come from training toughened and healthy, he had about him the air of a small child. He noticed a certain wildness in the eye, and he lay on the hard floor, as was his habit, in perfect comfort. He thought nothing. He felt nothing. He wished nothing.

Time passed as if he could compress and cancel it. Early-evening darkness began to make the white walls blue. He heard a crackling fire in the kitchen of the rooms next door, and imagined the shadows dancing there. Then he slept, departing.

On the mountain it was dreadfully cold. He huddled into himself against the wet silver clouds, and yet he smiled, happy to be once again on the summit. He thought of making an igloo, but remembered that he hadn't an ice saw. The wind began to build. If the storm continued, he would die. It would whittle him into a brittle wire, and then he would snap. The best he could do was to dig a trench with his ice hammers. He lay in the trench and closed his sleeves and hooded parka, drawing the shrouds tight. The wind came at him more and more fiercely. One gust was so powerful that it nearly lifted him out of the trench. He put in an ice piton, and attached his harness. Still the wind rose. It was difficult to breathe and nearly impossible to see. Any irregular surface whistled. The eye of the ice piton became a great siren. The zippers on his parka, the harness, the slings and equipment, all gave off musical tones, so that it was as if he were in a place with hundreds of tormented spirits.

The gray air fled past with breathtaking speed. Looking away from the wind, he had the impression of being propelled upward at unimaginable speed. Walls of gray sped by so fast that they glowed. He knew that if he were to look at the wind he would have the sense of hurtling forward in gravityless space.

And so he stared at the wind and its slowly pulsing gray glow. He did not know for how many hours he held that position. The rape of vision caused a host of delusions. He felt great momentum. He traveled until, eardrums throbbing with the sharpness of cold and wind, he was nearly dead, white as a candle, hardly able to breathe.

Then the acceleration ceased and the wind slowed. When, released from the great pressure, he fell back off the edge of the trench, he realized for the first time that he had been stretched tight on his line. He had never been so cold. But the wind was dying and the clouds were no longer a corridor through which he was propelled. They were, rather, a gentle mist which did not know quite what to do with itself. How would it dissipate? Would it rise to the stars, or would it fall in compression down into the valley below?

It fell; it fell all around him, downward like a lowering curtain. It fell in lines and stripes, always downward as if on signal, by command, in league with a directive force.

At first he saw just a star or two straight on high. But as the mist departed a flood of stars burst through. Roads of them led into infinity. Starry wheels sat in fiery white coronas. Near the horizon were the few separate gentle stars, shining out and turning clearly, as wide and round as planets. The air grew mild and warm. He bathed in it. He trembled. As the air became all clear and the mist drained away completely, he saw something which stunned him.

The Schreuderspitze was far higher than he had thought. It was hundreds of times higher than the mountains represented on the map he had seen in Munich. The Alps were to it not even foothills, not even rills. Below him was the purple earth, and all the great cities lit by sparkling lamps in their millions. It was a clear summer dawn and the weather was excellent, certainly June.

He did not know enough about other cities to make them out from the shapes they cast in light, but his eye

seized quite easily upon Munich. He arose from his trench
and unbuckled the harness, stepping a few paces higher
on the rounded summit. There was Munich, shining and
pulsing like a living thing, strung with lines of amber
light—light which reverberated as if in crystals, light
which played in many dimensions and moved about the
course of the city, which was defined by darkness at its
edge. He had come above time, above the world. The city
of Munich existed before him with all its time compressed.
As he watched, its history played out in repeating cycles.
Nothing, not one movement, was lost from the crystal.
The light of things danced and multiplied, again and
again, and yet again. It was all there for him to claim. It
was alive, and ever would be.

He knelt on one knee as in paintings he had seen of
explorers claiming a coast of the New World. He dared
close his eyes in the face of that miracle. He began to con-
centrate, to fashion according to will with the force of
stilled time a vision of those he had loved. In all their
bright colors, they began to appear before him.

He awoke as if shot out of a cannon. He went from lying
on his back to a completely upright position in an instant,
a flash, during which he slammed the floorboards energeti-
cally with a clenched fist and cursed the fact that he had
returned from such a world. But by the time he stood
straight, he was delighted to be doing so. He quickly
dressed, packed his bedding, and began to shuttle down
to the station and back. In three trips, his luggage was
stacked on the platform.

He bought a ticket for Munich, where he had not
been in many, many long months. He hungered for it, for
the city, for the boats on the river, the goods in the shops,
newspapers, the pigeons in the square, trees, traffic, even

arguments, even Herr Franzen. So much rushed into his mind that he hardly saw his train pull in.

He helped the conductor load his luggage into the baggage car, and he asked, "Will we change at Garmisch-Partenkirchen?"

"No. We go right through, direct to Munich," said the conductor.

"Do me a great favor. Let me ride in the baggage car."

"I can't. It's a violation."

"Please. I've been months in the mountains. I would like to ride alone, for the last time."

The conductor relented, and Wallich sat atop a pile of boxes, looking at the landscape through a Dutch door, the top of which was open. Trees and meadows, sunny and lush in June, sped by. As they descended, the vegetation thickened until he saw along the cinder bed slow-running black rivers, skeins and skeins of thorns darted with the red of early raspberries, and flowers, which had sprung up on the paths. The air was warm and caressing—thick and full, like a swaying green sea at the end of August.

They closed on Munich, and the Alps appeared in a sweeping line of white cloud-touched peaks. As they pulled into the great station, as sooty as it had ever been, he remembered that he had climbed the Schreuderspitze, by its most difficult route. He had found freedom from grief in the great and heart-swelling sight he had seen from the summit. He felt its workings and he realized that soon enough he would come once more into the world of light. Soon enough he would be with his wife and son. But until then (and he knew that time would spark ahead), he would open himself to life in the city, return to his former profession, and struggle at his craft.

Letters
from the
Samantha

These letters were recovered in good condition from the vault of the sunken *Samantha,* an iron-hulled sailing ship of one thousand tons, built in Scotland in 1879 and wrecked during the First World War in the Persian Gulf off Basra.

20 August, 1909, 20° 14′ 18″ S,
43° 51′ 57″ E
Off Madagascar

DEAR SIR:

Many years have passed since I joined the Green Star Line. You may note in your records and logs, if not, indeed, by memory, the complete absence of disciplinary action against me. During my command, the *Samantha* has been a trim ship on time. Though my subordinates sometimes complain, they are grateful, no doubt, for my firm rule and tidiness. It saves the ship in storms, keeps them healthy, and provides good training—even though they will be masters of steamships.

No other vessel of this line has been as punctual or well run. Even today we are a week ahead and our Madagascar wood will reach Alexandria early. Bound for London, the crew are happy, and though we sail the Mozambique Channel, they act as if we had just caught sight of Margate. There are no problems on this ship. But I must in conscience report an irregular incident for which I am ready to take full blame.

Half a day out of Androka, we came upon a sea so blue and casual that its waters seemed fit to drink. Though the wind was slight and we made poor time, we were elated by perfect climate and painter's colors, for off the starboard side Madagascar rose as green and tranquil as a well-watered palm, its mountains engraved by thrashing freshwater streams which beat down to the coast. A sweet upwelling breeze blew steadily from shore and confounded our square sails. Twenty minutes after noon, the lookout sighted a tornado on land. In the ship's glass I saw it, horrifying and enormous. Though at a great distance, its column appeared as thick as a massive tree on an islet in an atoll, and stretched at least 70 degrees upward from the horizon.

I have seen these pipes of windy fleece before. If there is sea nearby, they rush to it. So did this. When it became not red and black from soil and debris but silver and green from the water it drew, I began to tighten ship. Were the typhoon to have struck us directly, no preparation would have saved us. But what a shame to be swamped by high waves, or to be dismasted by beaten sea and wind. Hatches were battened as if for storm, minor sails furled, and the mainsail driven down half.

It moved back and forth over the sea in illegible patterning, as if tacking to changing winds. To our dismay, the distance narrowed. We were afraid, though every man on deck wanted to see it, to feel it, perhaps to ride its thick swirling waters a hundred times higher than our mast—higher than the peaks inland. I confess that I have wished to be completely taken up by such a thing, to be lifted into the clouds, arms and legs pinned in the stream. The attraction is much like that of phosphorescent seas, when glowing light and smooth swell are dangerously magnetic even for hardened masters of good ships. I have wanted to surrender to plum-colored seas, to know what one might find there naked and alone. But I have not, and will not.

Finally, we began to run rough water. The column was so high that we bent our heads to see its height, and the sound was greater than any engine, causing masts and spars to resonate like cords. Waves broke over the prow. Wind pushed us on, and the curl of the sea rushed to fill the depression of the waters. No more than half a mile off the starboard bow, the column veered to the west, crossing our path to head for Africa as rapidly as an express. Within minutes, we could not even see it.

As it crossed our bows, I veered in the direction from which it had come. It seemed to communicate a decisiveness of course, and here I took opportunity to evade. In doing so we came close to land. This was dangerous not only for the presence of reefs and shoals but because of the scattered debris. Trees as tall as masts and much thicker, roots sucked clean, lay in puzzlement upon the surface. Brush and vines were everywhere. The water was reddish brown from earth which had fallen from the cone. We were meticulously careful in piloting through this fresh salad, as a good ram against a solid limb would have been the end. Our cargo is hardwoods, and would have sunk us like granite. I myself straddled the sprit stays, pushing aside small logs with a boat hook and calling out trim to the wheel.

Nearly clear, we came upon a clump of tangled vegetation. I could not believe my eyes, for floating upon it was a large monkey, bolt upright and dignified. I sighted him first, though the lookout called soon after. On impulse, I set trim for the wavy mat and, as we smashed onto it, offered the monkey an end of the boat hook. When he seized it I was almost pulled in, for his weight is nearly equal to mine. I observed that he had large teeth, which appeared both white and sharp. He came close, and then took to the lines until he sat high on the topgallant. As he passed, his foot cuffed my shoulder and I could smell him.

My ship is a clean ship. I regretted immediately my gesture with the hook. We do not need the mysterious defecations of such a creature, or the threat of him in the rigging at night. But we could not capture him to throw him back into the sea and, even had we collared him, might not have been able to get him overboard without danger to ourselves. We are now many miles off the coast. It is dark, and he sits high off the deck. The night watch is afraid and requests that I fell him with my rifle. They have seen his sharp teeth, which he displays with much screaming and gesticulating when they near him in the rigging. I think he is merely afraid, and I cannot bring myself to shoot him. I realize that no animals are allowed on board and have often had to enforce this rule when coming upon a parrot or cat hidden belowdecks where some captains do not go. But this creature we have today removed from the sea is like a man, and he has ridden the typhoon. Perhaps we will pass a headland and throw him overboard on a log. He must eventually descend for want of food.

Then we will have our way. I will report further when the
matter is resolved, and assure you that I regret this breach
of regulations.

Yours & etc.,
SAMSON LOW
Master, S/V SAMANTHA

23 August, 1909, 10° 43′ 3″ S,
49° 5′ 27″ E
South of the Seychelles

DEAR SIR:
     We have passed the Channel and are heading
north-northeast, hoping to ride the summer monsoon. It
is shamefully hot, though the breeze is less humid than
usual. Today two men dropped from the heat but they resumed work by evening. Because we are on a homeward
tack, morale is at its best, or rather would be were it not
for that damned ape in the rigging. He has not come down,
and we have left behind his island and its last headland.
He will have to have descended by the time we breach passage between Ras Asir and Jazirat Abd al-Kuri. The mate
has suggested that there we throw him into the sea on a
raft, which the carpenter has already set about building.
He has embarked upon this with my permission, since
there is little else for him to do. It has been almost an
overly serene voyage and the typhoon caused no damage.
     The raft he designed is very clever and has become
a popular subject of discussion. It is about six feet by three
feet, constructed of spare pine dunnage we were about to
cast away when the typhoon was sighted. On each side

is an outrigger for stability in the swell. In the center is a box, in which is a seat. Flanking this box are several smaller ones for fruit, biscuit, and a bucket of fresh water, in case the creature should drift a long time on the sea. This probably will not be so; the currents off Ras Asir drive for the beach, and we have noted that dunnage is quickly thrown upon the strand. Nevertheless, the crew have added their own touch—a standard distress flag flying from a ten-foot switch. They do not know, but I will order it replaced by a banner of another color, so that a hapless ship will not endanger itself to rescue a speechless monkey.

The crew have divided into two factions—those who wish to have the monkey shot, and those who would wait for him to descend and then put him in his boat. I am with the latter, since I would be the huntsman, and have already mentioned my lack of enthusiasm for this. A delegation of the first faction protested. They claimed that the second faction comprised those who stayed on deck, that the creature endangered balance in the rigging, and that he produced an uncanny effect in his screeching and bellicose silhouettes, which from below are humorous but which at close range, they said, are disconcerting and terrifying.

Since I had not seen him for longer than a moment and wanted to verify their complaint, I went up. Though sixty years of age, I did not use the bosun's chair, and detest those masters who do. It is pharaonic, and smacks of days in my father's youth when he saw with his own eyes gentlemen in sedan chairs carried about the city. The sight of twenty men laboring to hoist a ship's rotund captain is simply Egyptian, and I will not have it. Seventy feet off the deck, a giddy height to which I have not ascended in years, I came even with the ape. The ship was passing a

boisterous sea and had at least a twenty-degree roll, which
flung the two of us from side to side like pendula.

I am not a naturalist, nor have we on board a book
of zoology, so the most I can do is to describe him. He
is almost my height (nearly five feet ten inches) and ap-
pears to be sturdily built. Feet and hands are human in
appearance except that they have a bulbous, skew, ar-
thritic look common to monkeys. He is muscular and covered with fine reddish-brown hair. One can see the whiteness of his tendons when he stretches an arm or leg. I have
mentioned the sharp, dazzling white teeth, set in rows like
a trap, canine and pointed. His face is curiously delicate,
and covered with orange hair leading to a snow-white
crown of fur. My breath nearly failed when I looked into
his eyes, for they are a bright, penetrating blue.

At first, he began to scream and swing as if he would
come at me. If he had, I would have fared badly. The sailors fear him, for there is no man on board with half his
strength, no man on the sea with a tenth his agility in the
ropes, and if there is a man with the glacierlike pinnacled
teeth, then he must be in a Scandinavian or Eastern European circus, for there they are fond of such things. To my
surprise, he stopped his pantomime and, with a gentle and
quizzical tilt of the head, looked me straight in the eyes.
I had been sure that as a man I could answer his gaze as
if from infallibility, and I calmly looked back. But he had
me. His eyes unset me, so that I nearly shook. From that
moment, he has not threatened or bared his teeth, but
merely rests near the top of the foremast. The crew have
attributed his conversion to my special power. This is flat-
tering, though not entirely, as it assumes my ability to
commune with an ape. Little do they suspect that it is I
and not the monkey who have been converted, although

to what I do not know. I am still thoroughly ashamed of
my indiscretion and the trouble arising from it. We will
get him and put him adrift off Ras Asir.

This evening, the cook grilled up some beef. I had
him thoroughly vent the galley and use a great many
herbs. The aroma was maddening. I sat in near-hypnotic
ease in a canvas chair on the quarterdeck, a glass of wine
in hand, as the heat fell to a cool breeze. We are all sunburnt and have been working hard, as the ape silently
watches, to trim regularly and catch the best winds. We
are almost in the full swift of the monsoon, and shortly
will ride it in all its speed. It was wonderful to sit on deck
and smell the herb-laden meat. The sea itself must have
been jealous. I had several men ready with cargo net and
pikes, certain that he would come down. We stared up at
him as if he were the horizon, waiting. He smelled the food
and agitated back and forth. Though he fretted, he did not
descend. Even when we ate we saw him shunting to and
fro on a yardarm. We left a dish for him away from us
but he did not venture to seize it. If he had, we would have
seized him.

From his impatience, I predict that tomorrow he will
surrender to his stomach. Then we will catch him and this
problem will be solved. I truly regret such an irregularity,
though it would be worthwhile if he could only tell us how
far he was lifted inside the silvered cone, and what it was
like.

Yours & etc.,
SAMSON LOW

25 August, 1909, 2° 13′ 10″ N,
51° 15′ 17″ E
Off Mogadishu

DEAR SIR:

Today he came down. After the last correspondence, it occurred to me that he might be vegetarian, and that though he was hungry, the meat had put him off. Therefore, I searched my memory for the most aromatic vegetable dish I know. In your service as a fourth officer, I called at Jaffa port, in Palestine, in January of 1873. We went up to Sfat, a holy town high in the hills, full of Jews and Arabs, quiet and mystical. There were so many come into that freezing velvet dome of stars that all hostelries were full. I and several others paid a small sum for private lodging and board. At two in the morning, after we had returned from Mt. Jermak, the Arabs made a hot lively fire from bundles of dry cyprus twigs, and in a great square iron pan heated local oil and herbs, in which they fried thick sections of potato. I have never eaten so well. Perhaps it was our hunger, the cold, the silence, being high in the mountains at Sfat, where air is like ether and all souls change. Today I made the cook follow that old receipt.

We had been in the monsoon for several hours, and the air was littered with silver sparks—apparitions of heat from a glittering afternoon. Though the sun was low, iron decks could not be tread. In the rigging, he appeared nearly finished, limp and slouching, an arm hanging without energy, his back bent. We put potatoes in a dish on the forecastle. He descended slowly, finally touching deck lightly and ambling to the bows like a spider, all limbs brushing the planks. He ate his fill, and we threw the net over him. We had expected a ferocious struggle, but his posture and expression were so peaceful that I ordered the net removed. Sailors stood ready with pikes, but he stayed in place. Then I approached him and extended my hand as if to a child.

In imitation, he put out his arm, looking much less fearsome. Without a show of teeth, in his tired state, crouched on all fours to half our heights, he was no more frightening than a hound. I led him to the stern and back again while the crew cheered and laughed. Then the mate took him, and then the entire hierarchy of the ship, down to the cabin boys, who are smaller than he and seemed to interest him the most. By dark, he had strolled with every member of the crew and was miraculously tame. But I remembered his teeth, and had him chained to his little boat.

He was comfortable there, surrounded by fruit and water (which he ate and drank methodically) and sitting on a throne of sorts, with half a dozen courtiers eager to look in his eyes and hold his obliging wrist. Mine is not the only London post in which he will be mentioned. Those who can write are describing him with great zeal. I have seen some of these letters. He has been portrayed as a "mad baboon," a "man-eating gorilla of horrible colors, muscled but as bright as a bird," a "pygmy man set down on the sea by miracle and typhoon," and as all manner of Latin names, each different from the others and incorrectly spelled.

Depending on the bend of the monsoon and whether it continues to run strongly, we will pass Ras Asir in three days. I thought of casting him off early but was implored to wait for the Cape. I relented, and in doing so was made to understand why those in command must stay by rules. I am sure, however, that my authority is not truly diminished, and when the ape is gone I will again tighten discipline.

I have already had the distress flag replaced by a green banner. It flies over the creature on his throne. Though in splendor, he is in chains and in three days' time will be on the sea once more.

Yours & etc.,
SAMSON LOW

28 August, 1909, 12° 4' 39" N,
50° 1' 2" E
North of Ras Asir

DEAR SIR:

A most alarming incident has occurred. I must report, though it is among the worst episodes of my command. This morning, I arose, expecting to put the ape over the side as we rounded Ras Asir at about eleven. (The winds have been consistently excellent and a northward breeze veering off the monsoon has propelled us as steadily as an engine.) Going out on deck, I discovered that his boat was nowhere to be seen. At first, I thought that the mate had already disposed of him, and was disappointed that we were far from the coast. Then, to my shock, I saw him sitting unmanacled atop the main cargo hatch.

I screamed at the mate, demanding to know what had happened to the throne (as it had come to be called). He replied that it had gone overboard during the twelve-to-four watch. I stormed below and got that watch out in a hurry. Though sleepy-eyed, they were terrified. I told them that if the guilty one did not come forth I would put them all in irons. My temper was short and I

could have struck them down. Two young sailors, as
frightened as if they were surrendering themselves to die,
admitted that they had thrown it over. They said they did
not want to see the ape put to drift.

They are in irons until we make Suez. Their names
are Mulcahy and Esper, and their pay is docked until they
are freed. As we rounded the Cape, cutting close in (for
the waters there are deep), we could see that though the
creature would have been immediately cast up on shore,
the shore itself was barren and inhospitable, and surely
he would have died there. My Admiralty chart does not
detail the inland topography of this area and shows only
a yellow tongue marked "Africa" thrusting into the Gulf
of Aden.

I can throw him overboard now or later. I do not
want to do it. I brought him on board in the first place.
There is nothing with which to fashion another raft. We
have many tons of wood below, but not a cubic foot of
it is lighter than water. The wind is good and we are making for the Bab al-Mandab, where we will pass late tomorrow afternoon—after that, the frustrating run up the Red
Sea to the Canal.

The mate suggests that we sell him to the Egyptians.
But I am reluctant to make port with this in mind, as it
would be a victory for the two in chains and in the eyes
of many others. And we are not animal traders. If he
leaves us at sea the effects of his presence will be invalidat-
ed, we will touch land with discipline restored, and I will
have the option of destroying these letters, though everything here has been entered in short form in the log. I have
ordered him not to be fed, but they cast him scraps. I must
get back my proper hold on the ship.

Yours & etc.,
SAMSON LOW

30 August, 1909, 15° 49′ 30″ N,
41° 5′ 32″ E
Red Sea off Massawa

DEAR SIR:

I have been felled by an attack of headaches. Never before has this happened. There is pressure in my skull enough to burst it. I cannot keep my balance; my eyes roam and I am drunk with pain. For the weary tack up the Red Sea I have entrusted the mate with temporary command, retiring to my cabin with the excuse of heat prostration. I have been in the Red Sea time and again but have never felt apprehension that death would follow its heat. We have always managed. To the east, the mountains of the Hijaz are so dry and forbidding that I have seen sailors look away in fright.

The ape has begun to suffer from the heat. He is listless and ignored. His novelty has worn off (with the heat as it is) and no one pays him any attention. He will not go belowdecks but spends most of the day under the canvas sun shield, chewing slowly, though there is nothing in his mouth. It is hot there—the light so white and uncompromising it sears the eyes. I have freed his champions from irons and restored their pay. By this act I have won over the crew and caused the factions to disappear. No one thinks about the ape. But I dare not risk a recurrence of bad feeling and have decided to cast him into the sea. Where we found him, a strong seaward current would have carried him to the open ocean. Here, at least, he can make the shore, although it is the most barren coast on earth. But who would have thought he might survive the typhoon? He has been living beyond his time. To be picked up and whirled at incomprehensible speed, carried for miles above the earth where no man has ever been, and thrown into the sea is a death sentence. If he survived that, perhaps he can survive Arabian desert.

His expression is neither sad nor fierce. He looks like an old man, neutral to the world. In the last two days he has become the target of provocation and physical blows. I have ordered this stopped, but a sailor will sometimes throw a nail or a piece of wood at him. We shall soon be rid of him.

Yesterday we came alongside another British ship, the *Stonepool,* of the Dutch Express Line. On seeing the ape, they were envious. What is it, their captain asked, amazed at its coloring. I replied that he was a Madagascar ape we had fished from the sea, and I offered him to them, saying he was as tame as a dog. At first, they wanted him. The crew cried out for his acceptance, but the captain demurred, shaking his head and looking into my eyes as if he were laughing at me. "Damn!" I said, and went below without even a salute at parting.

My head aches. I must stop. At first light tomorrow, I will toss him back.

Yours & etc.,
SAMSON LOW

3 September, 1909
Suez

DEAR SIR:
The morning before last I went on deck at dawn. The ape was sitting on the main hatch, his eyes upon me from

the moment I saw him. I walked over to him and extended my arm, which he would not take in his customary manner. I seized his wrist, which he withdrew. However, as he did this I laid hold of the other wrist, and pulled him off the hatch. He did not bare his teeth. He began to scream. Awakened by this, most of the crew stood in the companionways or on deck, silently observing.

He was hard to drag, but I towed him to the rail. When I took his other arm to hoist him over, he bared his teeth with a frightening shriek. Everyone was again terrified. The teeth must be six inches long.

He came at me with those teeth, and I could do nothing but throttle him. With my hands on his throat, his arms were free. He grasped my side. I felt the pads of his hands against my ribs. I had to tolerate that awful sensation to keep hold of his throat. No man aboard came close. He shrieked and moaned. His eyes reddened. My response was to tighten my hold, to end the horror. I gripped so hard that my own teeth were bared and I made sounds similar to his. He put his hands around my neck as if to strangle me back, but I had already taken the inside position and, despite his great strength, lessened the power of his grip merely by lifting my arms against his. Nevertheless he choked me. But I had a great head start. We held this position for long minutes, sweating, until his arms dropped and his body convulsed. In rage, I threw him by the neck into the sea, where he quickly sank.

Some of the crew have begun to talk about him as if he were about to be canonized. Others see him as evil. I assembled them as the coasts began to close on Suez and the top of the sea was white and still. I made my views clear, for in years of command and in a life on the sea I have learned much. I felt confident of what I told them.

He is not a symbol. He stands neither for innocence nor for evil. There is no parable and no lesson in his coming and going. I was neither right nor wrong in bringing him aboard (though it was indeed incorrect) or in what I later did. We must get on with the ship's business. He does not stand for a man or men. He stands for nothing. He was an ape, simian and lean, half sensible. He came on board, and now he is gone.

Yours & etc.,
SAMSON LOW

Martin
Bayer

By September, 1916, the hotels on Long Island's eastern extremity were in dire straits. Southampton marked the limit of fashionability, because military camps, whalers, a few remaining Indians, and the thinness of the land projecting unescorted into open ocean kept most people from the one or two resorts near the Amagansett beaches. People had avoided the shore since the sinking of the *Lusitania,* for it was rumored that the Germans were going to use gas and germ warfare against the Atlantic Coast. Autumn was approaching, and all but the very rich and unemployed were pulled back to Manhattan and Brooklyn as if by electromagnetic force. The sea was cold and bright.

Mr. Bayer had seen a newspaper advertisement describing a hotel as splendid as a palace of Byzantium, overlooking a regal, breathtaking prospect of savage sea—with extraordinary conveniences, with a garden close of tall oaks and fireflies—offering ten days' room and board to a family of four at a hundred and fifty dollars. He had forfeited a vacation that summer because business was booming and demanded full attention. It was especially delightful to know that by traveling in the off-season he could bank a hundred and fifty of the three hundred dollars budgeted for a holiday, during a time when he was making so much money anyway. Of course the hotel was a gamble, but one fine morning in Manhattan, when summer's last colors were sharpened by a blast of fall air galloping down the Hudson from Canada, they set out in their automobile for ten days at Amagansett. The air was so clear and enlivening that they wondered why they were headed into the country just as the heat was finally dying.

When Mr. Bayer and Martin had lashed canvas over the suitcases and automotive-repair apparatus, Martin's sixteen-year-old sister, Lydia, got in the front seat with an expression of determination and dread.

"Lydia!" said Mr. Bayer. "Ride in the back with your mother."

"That's right," said Martin, pompously.

"Martin, you shut up. Lydia, in the back."

"No," she said. "I want to ride in the front."

"Lydia, please come in the back," said Mrs. Bayer. "The front is for Daddy and Martin, in case of a puncture."

"No." Every time she said "No," the word got shorter.

"Lydia, Daddy says you'd better get in back or—"

"Shut up, Martin. Lydia, darling, get in back or we don't go to Amagansett."

"I don't *want* to go to Amagansett," she said. "We'll be the only people there. Why can't I ride in the front?"

"Martin rides in the front. He's a boy."

"But he's only ten."

"Ten and three-fifths," said Martin.

"Lydia, Lydia," said Mrs. Bayer. Then she leaned forward and touched her daughter's cheek. Lydia was extremely beautiful, with a warm, gentle face. She stood up, got out, slammed the door, got in the back, slammed the door, and stared at the second floor of their house. Her

reddened face and neck and incipient tears made her even
more beautiful, and her mother embraced her while Martin and Mr. Bayer, nearly chuckling over their victory,
climbed in the front and began the driving.

Martin was in charge of the emergency brake, the
gasoline gauge, the water temperature, and cleaning the
windshield—which he thought was a "winsheel." In a
breakdown, he was the warning dummy, rag carrier, and
nut holder. Even though Lydia wanted these jobs, she
would not have taken them had they been offered. But
Martin was extremely proud of the responsibility, just as
he was proud to stand with the mannequins in his father's
store window, looking grave, as he thought a young mer-
cantile employee should when in public view. But he hated
to wash dishes or take out the garbage, and would disappear after dinner as if composed of the rarest gas—better
to be beaten up by the Irish ruffians who terrorized the
Jews than to take out garbage. This was mainly because
the Irish ruffians never did beat up the Jews. Instead, they
described it in such convincing detail that the Jews ran
home overbrimming with the living English—"He
smashed my face, bashed my belly, and splintered my Jew
bones"—and the memory of a fight that had really never
been.

They drove at 23 m.p.h. down the avenues to the
Brooklyn Bridge. Martin glanced in the windows of
sepia-colored tenements full of stretching people new to
morning. There was still some sense of wilderness left in
the city, in the brown and the dust, in the freshness of the
earth overturned in excavation, in the farmlike emerald
beauty of the Park. Once, his father had awakened him
at four in the morning just to walk in the streets. They
wound through fresh squares and down empty boulevards
into the commercial district, where, at five, the markets

were feverishly active. Martin was in an airless daze, though on that unusually warm March morning the air was wet and mild. The last drunk was expelled from the most riotous bar with a thunderclap and he wheeled through the doors and hit the sidewalk, rolling about like a ball bearing. Martin thought the ladies of the night were early-rising shopgirls and devoted nurses. Father and son passed countless gleaming fish on ice-covered tables, barrels of herring, vegetables still fresh and spotted with earth from Hudson Valley farms. They went into a workmen's cafe. It was the only time Martin had ever drunk coffee. The proprietor put so much extra milk in it that he had to charge Mr. Bayer another nickel, but Martin didn't know, and, despite his size, tried to blend with the crowd by pretending that he was a grown man.

They drove at 23 m.p.h. because their mechanic had told them that if they didn't the engine would burn out. Martin liked the way the engine sounded, rolling over and around itself like a player piano. The sound of machines was like the rising of the sun on a winter morning, full of promise, relief, and lightheartedness. Martin liked so many things that he could not open his eyes without a pleasant inrush. And he was prone to fits of laughter. Once, they had dressed him up and taken him to a concert hall near the Park. Martin thought it was wonderful—the airy echoing ballroom, a view of dark-green citified trees, a mixture of expensive perfumes, and miles of silver trays with a thousand pounds of what Martin termed "complexly baked sculpture cookies." After eating thirty or forty of these and quenching his thirst with four or five cups of champagne punch, Martin thought the world was a paradise. He took his seat while the musicians tuned their instruments. He was just beginning to fall asleep when an enormous fat woman suddenly appeared from be-

hind a curtain and began to scream and squeak. Her teeth
stuck way out of her mouth, and after the especially long
and voluminous squeaks, she looked proud and delighted.
At first, Martin was dumbfounded. Then he began to giggle, keeping it down until the muscles in his throat and
abdomen felt as if they were sweating fire. The pain and
tension were such that he started to get serious, when
Lydia, afraid of being deathly embarrassed, decided to in-
flict a minor torture on him to stop the oncoming explosion. This she did by reaching from behind and driving
her fingers into his ribs. Overflowing, caught by surprise,
and got from behind, Martin shrieked with such force that
people all around him jumped in their seats. A storm of
laughter then issued from him. Unable to catch his breath,
he rolled on the floor in such enviable enjoyment that the
rest of the hall found it wonderfully amusing, even when
Mr. Bayer swatted him and carried him, still doubled
over, out the French doors into the greenery.

Recognizing her role in the disaster, and that it had
cost Martin his allowance and several outings, Lydia took
him to the aquarium. Of course he was delighted, but, as
they tiptoed through the slimy galleries, he thought she
was crazy. "How do you know they're looking at you?"
he asked.

"How do I know *who's* looking?" replied Lydia.

"I don't care if people look at *me*," said Martin, "but
you think boys look at you all the time. That's why you
walk around like a statue." He imitated her straight oblivious stare, which made her look as if she had a neck injury,
and, not understanding her lovely self-consciousness, he
was soon lost in consideration of green water, gliding
sharks, giant sea turtles jetting along with glinting paddle
fins, the humidity on the face of the jewel-like tanks, and
the feeling of the water's mass and weight behind the thick

glass. He had worn a blue sailor suit, and he had dashed
from place to place.

On the Brooklyn side, once the Bayers had viewed
Manhattan from the air and seen a landscape of chimneys
and brown stone, they passed a faraway group of wan
naked swimmers scattered at the foot of piers and em-
bankments (as if they had been thrown there) and soaring
from towers and walls into the swirling water. Martin
stared at the swimmers with a near-pickled eye. The pleasure was beckoning and indefatigable, but he leaned back
to watch the trees passing overhead on a river of blue. He
remembered how in winter they went up on Riverside
Drive to watch little steam ferries charge across the
ice-packed North River, setting out in a puff of white crystal breath, rolling across the cold blue water.

The hotel at Amagansett was a large, airy white frame
house standing in the deep green of potato fields that ran
to a bluff overlooking an Arabian stretch of dunes and the
blinding sea. Martin and Lydia walked to the water each
day to swim and jump down the cool sides of the dunes.
The sea was achingly cold, so their parents often ignored
the beach in favor of sitting on the porch. In the green
and the silence, they seemed to be happy just rocking back
and forth in beads of cascading sun, their faces relaxed
and content.

For the first time, Martin discovered that he carried
a store of strong memories which emerged bright and clear
in his eyes and gave him access to a world of random and
sudden images as beautiful as the upwelling of music. He
was chasing a horse in the pasture behind the hotel. The
hotelkeeper, a portly Dane named Friebourg, had told
Martin that if he could saddle the colt in the back field
he could ride him. "Before you saddle him," the Dane had

said with amusement, "you'll have to catch him, and that, little boy, could take a long time. I will sit here and watch, for this will be better than the vaudeville." Martin had not liked the Dane's patronizing attitude, and was determined to catch the colt.

The colt looked at him with the confidence and superiority of a dentist, knowing that after a little bit of fun the creature on tiny legs who had come to capture him would soon be incoherent and exhausted. It was just that way. Martin coaxed him with sweet language, fake smiles, hoarse rhetoric, careful commands, invigorated threats, and pleas for mercy. Nibbling the grass until Martin stealthily approached, breathing hot and heavy, lasso in hand, the colt then flew to another extreme of the field. Martin ran himself silly. Had the colt thrust his neck into the noose, Martin would not have had the strength to hold on, after two hours of the chase. Meanwhile, beyond the clover, the porch had filled with his family and the Friebourgs—the Dane himself, whose laughter could be heard from the pasture; Mrs. Friebourg, a silent hardworking woman; their daughter, Christiana, a girl just a year or two older than Lydia; and an ever-present, cut-glass gallon pitcher of beer.

In exhaustion and embarrassment Martin discovered that his defeat gave rise to splendid pictures—that the mahogany color of the horse billowed into a world of darkwood city interiors and the dappled shapes of figures within. An exhalation of breath and a dizzy glance at a lone white cloud, riding far off, locked into a tableau of winter in Manhattan—the breath of horses in snow, dark-blue water off the Battery, a shadow across a cold field in which stood a charcoal-limned tree. These frames appeared and he felt the city behind him in a cloud of heat, as if it were a living body like his own. Even though Mr. Friebourg laughed, Martin continued to chase the horse, comforting himself by enjoying the color in a world he saw rapidly blooming and dying as if it were running the gates of a rigid metal machine, remembering all the while the sadness he felt in the frozen images of a motion picture when it ran improperly and crippled. That night he went to bed early and sore. Mrs. Bayer put mayapple vinegar on his legs for the sunburn, and he fell asleep listening to the breeze in contest with a lissome Norway pine.

The next morning, Martin was outside the hotel at five-thirty, furiously building what he called a "wind indicator," which was a tangle of sticks, flags, strings, and tin cans, designed to sound a different tone for each of the four prime directions of wind. After several hours, it actually worked, though there was no telling what would have happened had the steady south wind changed its course.

Finally, Christiana Friebourg passed by (he had built it mainly for her benefit, imagining that she was watching every step) and asked, "What is that silly thing, Martin? Don't you think you should clean it up before Father gets back from the village?"

Martin was stung nearly to breathlessness, but he managed to reply, "It's a wind indicator, so I can always know which way the wind is blowing, even if I'm inside with my eyes closed."

"What does it matter?"

"It matters," answered Martin, though he did not know why it did. "It matters." Then they both turned at the sound of an automobile coming down the road that led across the potato fields. It was not Mr. Friebourg, for he had gone to town in the wagon.

They watched in silence until a drab-colored car with a Marine colonel and his orderly, a lieutenant, pulled up to the hotel. There was an emergency camp at Montauk, across a savage spit of sand and scrub which gave the impression of a fortress and had the air of war, battles, and extremities. Vulnerable on both sides, it was at one point only about five hundred feet wide between the sea and the sound. This was called Napeague Neck. Hundreds of Marines lived on a clifftop above the ocean and practiced gunnery and drills, standing on the sand or knee-deep in low grasses, staring out upon a sea over which they imagined a cold and dark field of battle. When fall closed in, the colonel drove about in his car, looking for families to receive his men for Sunday dinners. It was lonely out there. The approaching autumn was full of fright, as if regenerative nature put to rest were linked to the future of their battalion—which they were sure was destined for France. That morning, it was arranged that the officers would eat at the hotel. The lieutenant evidently knew Christiana, for they spoke by the side of the car as the colonel wrote checks to Friebourg. Martin was awed by the lieutenant's Sam Browne belt and field hat, not to mention the pistol, khaki puttees, lanyard, gold bars, and, most of all, the man's speech. He was from South Carolina. To Martin's delight, he was comfortable and fluent in his dialect. The lieutenant could not open his mouth without conjuring, for Martin, Martin's idea of the South—burned mansions amid coconut palms, at the foot of which speedy alligators with dangling tongues ran as fast as greyhounds in pursuit of bonneted children and screaming slaves.

When the two men left in the puffing automobile, Martin felt uncomfortable. He thought they were very high and brave, and he might even have wanted to be like them, but the equilibrium of the place had disappeared. They were attractive precisely because they were subject to the caprice of war. They had about them the uncertainty of a frontier, and were unsettling. He did not want them to come on Sunday, especially since Lydia had been magnetized like a needle on a lodestone, and suddenly looked as if she knew something that no one else knew. For Martin, the Marines were like night and cold.

But that Sunday was like summer, and, in ranging the far stretches of beach in search of landed sharks or the magnificent sight of a Coast Guardsman galloping his mount along the water's edge, Martin forgot about threats from outside. Even looking to the ocean's horizon, he did not sense beyond the rim the haunting battles which, at other times, were felt by all as if they were the approaching storms of the hurricane season. That day was hot and blue, with a magnificent cold wind.

Almost part of the landscape, Martin wandered down the beach. He wanted to go as far east as he could and then turn to make his way home. A breeze came from the sea, tossing spray off the tips of clear waves. Beach and surrounding duneland were abandoned to autumn. Martin crested the top of a high dune and looked over a pine forest and the multiple intrusions of sounds, bays, inlets, and broken spits with the risen water surging through to make pools in the midst of scrub trees. On the partly sand-covered macadam road, he saw the Marine colonel's empty automobile.

They must be swimming, thought Martin, or scouting the coast. Then his heart jumped as he saw two figures disappear beyond a wavelike hill of roseate voluted sand. He ran to join them, breathless and afraid, and, although he did not hesitate long enough to discover why, he felt drawn inevitably into something that he suspected would make him appear foolish. When he came near to where they had been, he stayed low among the sharp grasses. Then he felt as if he had come upon a momentous and terrible truth. The young lieutenant and Christiana Frie-

bourg were swimming together in the sea, having left their
clothing on the beach. The air was dry and it snapped at
wave crests. The lieutenant and Christiana appeared and
disappeared over the plane of white beach as they were
lifted entwined and turning in the waves. They kissed, and
seemed to dance buoyantly, like swans, in a field of azure.
They never wet their hair, and always were grasped together and revolving. Christiana threw back her head. Her
body, shining from seawater, was nearly as glossy as the
brine.

Not wanting to be seen, Martin crept in prodigious
low-coursed leaps to a channel between the hills, and ran
toward the hotel convinced that the only way he could
save himself from a fate unknown at the hands of the lieutenant was to pretend that he had spent the entire day in
the opposite direction. He ran for miles, appearing at the
hotel as heated as if he had been firing boilers. For about
fifteen minutes Mrs. Bayer had watched him running in
from the east. "Where have you been, Martin?"

"I was down there," he said, pointing straight to the
west. In a frenzy he went inside and opened a box of ster-
eoscopic views, shuffling them for an hour without memory of a single scene, until Christiana entered casually and
went to the kitchen to help her mother. Martin was shaking, sure that she had found him out. How he pitied poor
Friebourg and feared for Lydia, since there was no way
for him to protect her from the possession which had come
over Christiana. When he imagined Lydia naked in the
waves, spinning in ecstatic circles with the tall Marine, he
blacked out (or perhaps fell asleep) and remembered nothing until the long shadows of Sunday afternoon and a mad
rush in the kitchen told him that the Marine was really
going to appear, that he would have the daring and contempt to sit at table with the fallen Christiana and her par-

ents. How could anyone be that cruel? And Christiana seemed so happy. Even Martin's sparkling images gave him no comfort. He prayed that dinner would be short, war break out, and the Marines suffer immediate recall. When they were late, he felt moments of relief in imagining that they were already out on the dark hurricane-covered sea, pushing without any lights toward France and oblivion.

The Marines arrived at early evening—the lieutenant, the colonel, a major, and two other lieutenants. Almost in panic, Martin tried to pull Lydia away from the gathering. He went about, shifty-eyed and breathing hard, attempting to separate her from the Marines. "Lydia! Lydia!" he cried, holding up a dime book. "Read me about Captain Strumpet!" Everyone looked at him in the most peculiar fashion—especially his mother and father, since in normal times Martin would not allow anyone even to touch the Captain Strumpet book.

"Martin," his mother said, "let's not have another Turkish Carpet." No one except the Bayers themselves understood this, and they were glad that it seemed to quiet Martin down. Mrs. Bayer had been referring to Martin's punishment after they had all gone to buy a Turkish carpet at a fancy rug showroom in one of the new skyscrapers. As they entered the elevator, Martin had come face to face with the elevator boy—who was really a midget.

"Fourteen, please," Mr. Bayer said.

Martin took an immediate dislike to this fake boy. He did not approve of the uniform that made the little man look like an organ-grinder's monkey or a jockey in military dress, so he said, "I'll take seven."

"No," said Mr. Bayer. "Don't pay any attention to him." He glowered at Martin, and the elevator boy sneered triumphantly. On the third floor, they stopped to pick up a diva wrapped in tubular white furs.

"Eleven, please," Martin said in falsetto.

The elevator boy tipped his little cakebox hat at the diva, but she said, "Take me to five."

"Nine," said Martin, moving to the back of the car to avoid his father.

"Fourteen," repeated Mr. Bayer.

"Eight!" shouted Martin.

The fake boy was so confused that he had to halt the elevator and ask each person in turn what floor was desired. Later, after they had bought the rug, Martin sweetened his victory by running down fourteen flights of stairs and pushing the elevator call on each floor.

An ocher-colored cloth covered the table, and to the side was a marble-topped cart laden with champagne and bowls of fruit, and shining from the clear electric lights. Christiana stood behind this cart, in a beautiful dress. Her hair was drawn up and this full exposure made her look a bit awkward and sad, but when the lieutenant came in he stared at her gentle imperfect face as if there were nothing finer in the world. He helped her open the champagne, which overflowed onto the marble. They then drank toasts to Britain, France, the Marines, and the U.S. Even Martin had two glasses, but held off at that for fear of another concert-hall disaster. He looked out into the smoky darkness and the rows of trees, thinking of nearby farmyards and their populations of raucous, jovial hogs, sarcastic chickens, and bleating lambs. He ate large amounts of black bread and smoked fish.

One of the Marines went out to the automobile and returned with his guitar, on which he played exciting Spanish songs. He had left the door open, and before they knew it a swarm of flashing insects circled the lights. In the middle of September there was always a renaissance of summer insects. They came in waves from the brown grasses and the silent, still forests, their movements urgent and overheated, as if they knew that soon nights as clear as spirit would fell them and they would quickly become only crackling shells among the frail leaves.

It seemed to Martin that the lieutenant paid excessive attention to Christiana. Before dinner they stayed together in a corner, on a velvet divan, talking as if being close and in love were a patent on the world. He pulled out her chair when they sat down. Martin felt less and less apprehensive, for the lieutenant seemed not to be an exploiter or a philanderer but, rather, a good man acting from his heart. This made Martin almost carefree as he began, like the others, to enjoy the lieutenant's and Christiana's mutual infatuation. The young soldier noticed that he was drawing Martin's attention and, almost pained to look away from Christiana, turned to him and asked, "What do you want to be when you grow up?"

Martin reddened and stared at the bronze buttons on which were engraved a globe and an anchor. He had never known how to answer that question. "I want to be a painter," he said.

"And live in a garret!" boomed out Mr. Friebourg.

"And live in a *palace*," said Martin, strongly, besieged from all sides. A vision of a life of colors came to him, and he saw himself laying-on the smooth lateral white of snowfields, beyond which a blue river cut straight as a rail and steamers were strokes of black, gold, and brown followed by billows of icy mist.

"Mr. Bellows doesn't live in a garret," said Lydia. "If Martin says he wants to be a painter, then he *will* be a painter." Martin nodded his head in approval, of course, and there was silence but for the cicadas outside.

Mrs. Friebourg burst out of the kitchen with a tureen of soup. They drank beer as they pulled apart boiled lobsters and burned their fingers on ears of hot corn. Though the Marines got their own clams and did a lot of surf casting, they seldom had lobster. Perhaps because of the beer and the struggle against the lobsters, talk turned to war. The major had studied closely reports of the fighting, and he opposed the colonel and the lieutenants. "This war," he said, "is by no means like others. Never before have machine guns, aeroplanes, and mines been such a threat to survival in battle. I fear that the casualty rates will eventually make those of the War of the Rebellion seem charitable."

"Nonsense," said the colonel. "What about Gatling guns in the War of the Rebellion and after?"

"Never used in large-scale battles, sir," answered the major.

"I think you're exaggerating," said a lieutenant. "For in open country we should be able to outflank the trenches and barbed wire. When the U.S. enters the War, its character will change."

"Indeed," said the major.

Mrs. Bayer interjected. "Do you think we *will* enter the War, Colonel?"

"As certainly as history, Madam. The Germans cannot sink American ships with impunity, and there are political and moral reasons which demand our participation. I believe that with the spring we will declare war, and I hope that this battalion will be among the first to go to France."

Talk of war vanished as quickly as it had come, when Mrs. Friebourg brought dishes of ice cream garnished with waffle cookies and sprigs of mint. Martin looked at his portion and turned to his father with an air of offended innocence. "Take this leaf out of my ice cream," he commanded.

"Why can't you take it out yourself, Martin?" asked Mr. Bayer.

"I didn't put it there."

"I didn't, either."

"I put the leaf, Martin," said Mrs. Friebourg. "We always had mint with the ice cream in Denmark. Do you know what is Denmark?"

"Of course I do," answered Martin. "I've been there."

"You have?" Mrs. Bayer asked, knowing that Martin had never been out of New York State. "When?"

"Before I was born," Martin said, matter-of-factly. "I remember," he continued, closing his eyes and tilting his face like a medium (he even grasped the table with both hands), "I remember . . . butter . . . lots of butter. And little herring boats in the ocean, turning on the waves. They had beaches there, just like here, but not as big. And there was a circus that I went to; it was very small, they played violins, there was a tiger, the costumes were old-fashioned, and the tent was lit by candles."

Martin opened his eyes. He had made up the butter and the herring boats, but he had really seen the circus. It had come at him from nowhere, and was very real—he had heard the music and seen the tent gaily lit by candles.

"Yes," said Mrs. Friebourg, "I have seen a circus like that," and, for a moment, the room was silent.

Then they got up and had tea, and danced to a player piano and the guitar. The air was cool and beautiful, washed with white, the fields quiet and settled after a summer of growing. The lieutenant danced with Christiana.

They were in love. Then, when everyone was red from the dancing and delighted by the near-autumn evening, the lieutenant asked Mr. Friebourg to go out on the porch. Soon Mrs. Friebourg and her daughter followed. The remaining military and the Bayers did not know what to make of it. When the Friebourgs returned, they were beaming. Perhaps it was because the lieutenant was a handsome young man who had gone to university and whose family was known in the South. Perhaps it was because he was wealthy. Perhaps it was because they saw that he and their daughter were genuinely in love. They went to the marble-topped cart and poured champagne. Unable to restrain herself, Mrs. Friebourg said, in her thick Scandinavian accent, "Christiana and Lieutenant Thomson are to be married!" Lydia gasped with pleasure. Everyone smiled, and the Marines made little bows. The prospective bride and bridegroom were young and beautiful.

Martin's painted scenes danced before his eyes. He remembered the gaiety of the azure water and how unknowing he had felt. But then a picture of uniforms appeared (of course, it was easy) and he saw something in the bright colors which was sad. As the adults gathered to congratulate the lieutenant and his bride-to-be, Martin stepped out on the porch where they had watched him, a little boy, foolishly chasing a horse. The picture inside, through the large window, was active and full of life. He saw the lovers on an azure sea, and he saw white foam tossed by dry winds. He saw them perfectly in love, innocent. Christiana was again behind the marble, serving happily. The lieutenant was tall and stood like a prince.

On glowing boards flooded with moonlight he stared at the fields and could hear the ocean beyond. It was like an end-of-summer dream. But despite the iridescence of the moon, and the delight of middle September's solid blue fields alive with crickets, Martin saw frightening scenes and sad scenes, of ships fighting darkly across a hurricane-covered sea.

North Light

—A RECOLLECTION
IN THE
PRESENT TENSE

We are being held back. We are poised at a curve in the road on the southern ridge of a small valley. The sun shines from behind, illuminating with flawless light the moves and countermoves of several score tanks below us. For a long time, we have been absorbed in the mystery of matching the puffs of white smoke from tank cannon with the sounds that follow. The columns themselves move silently: only the great roar rising from the battle proves it not to be a dream.

A man next to me is deeply absorbed in sniffing his wrist. "What are you doing?" I ask.

"My wife," he says. "I can still smell her perfume on my wrist, and I taste the taste of her mouth. It's sweet."

We were called up this morning. The war is two days old. Now it is afternoon, and we are being held back—even though our forces below are greatly outnumbered. We are being held back until nightfall, when we will have a better chance on the plain; for it is packed with tanks, and we have only two old half-tracks. They are loaded with guns—it is true—but they are lightly armored, they are slow, and they present high targets. We expect to move at dusk or just before. Then we will descend on the road into the valley and fight amid the shadows. No one wants this: we all are terrified.

The young ones are frightened because, for most of them, this is the first battle. But their fear is not as strong as the blood which is rising and fills their chests with anger and strength. They have little to lose, being, as they are, only eighteen. They look no more frightened than members of a sports team before an important match: it is that kind of fear, for they are responsible only to themselves.

Married men, on the other hand, are given away by their eyes and faces. They are saying to themselves, "I must not die; I *must not die.*" They are remembering how they used to feel when they were younger; and they know that they have to fight. They may be killed, but if they don't fight they will surely be killed, because the slow self-made fear which demands constant hesitation is the most efficient of all killers. It is not the cautious who die, but the overcautious. The married men are trying to strike an exact balance between their responsibility as soldiers, their fervent desire to stay alive, and their only hope—which is to go into battle with the smooth, courageous, trancelike movements that will keep them out of trouble. Soldiers who do not know how (like dancers or mountain climbers) to let their bodies think for them are very liable to be killed. There is a flow to hard combat; it is not (as it has often been depicted) entirely chance or entirely skill. A thousand signals and signs speak to you, much as in music. And what a sad moment it is when you must, for one reason or another, ignore them. The married men fear this moment. We should have begun hours ago. Being held back is bad luck.

"What time is it?" asks one of the young soldiers. Someone answers him.

"Fourteen hundred." No one in the Israeli Army except high-ranking officers (colonels, generals—and we have here no colonels or generals) tells time in this fashion.

"What are you, a general?" asks the young soldier. Everyone laughs, as if this were funny, because we are scared. We should not be held back like this.

Another man, a man who is close to fifty and is worrying about his two sons who are in Sinai, keeps on looking at his watch. It is expensive and Japanese, with a black dial. He looks at it every minute to see what time it is, because he has actually forgotten. If he were asked what the time was, he would not be able to respond without checking the watch, even though he has done so fifty times in the last hour. He too is very afraid. The sun glints off the crystal and explodes in our eyes.

As younger men who badly wanted to fight, we thought we knew what courage was. Now we know that courage is the forced step of going into battle when you want anything in the world but that, when there is every reason to stay out, when you have been through all the tests, and passed them, and think that it's all over. Then the war hits like an artillery shell and you are forced to be eighteen again, but you can't be eighteen again; not with the taste of your wife's mouth in your mouth, not with the smell of her perfume on your wrists. The world turns upside down in minutes.

How hard we struggle in trying to remember the easy courage we once had. But we can't. We must either be brave in a different way, or not at all. What is that way? How can we fight like seasoned soldiers when this morning we kissed our children? There is a way, hidden in the history of war. There must be, for we can see them fighting in the valley; and, high in the air, silver specks are dueling in a dream of blue silence.

Why are we merely watching? To be restrained this way is simply not fair. A quick entrance would get the fear over with, and that would help. But, then again, in the

Six Day War, we waited for weeks while the Egyptian Army built up against us. And then, after that torture, we burst out and we leapt across the desert, sprinting, full of energy and fury that kept us like dancers—nimble and absorbed—and kept us alive. That is the secret: You have to be angry. When we arrived on the ridge this morning, we were anything but angry. Now we are beginning to get angry. It is our only salvation. We are angry because we are being held back.

We swear, and kick the sides of the half-tracks. We hate the voice on our radio which keeps telling us to hold to our position. We hate that man more than we hate the enemy, for now we want engagement with the enemy. We are beginning to crave battle, and we are getting angrier, and angrier, because we know that by five o'clock we will be worn out. They should let us go now.

A young soldier who has been following the battle, through binoculars, screams. "God!" he says. "Look! Look!"

The Syrians are moving up two columns of armor that will overwhelm our men on the plain below. The sergeant gets on the radio, but from it we hear a sudden waterfall of talk. Holding the microphone in his hand, he listens with us as we discover that they know. They are demanding more air support.

"What air support?" we ask. There is no air-to-ground fighting that we can see. As we watch the Syrians approach, our hearts are full of fear for those of us below. How did our soldiers know? There must be spotters or a patrol somewhere deep in, high on a hill, like us. What air support? There are planes all over the place, but not here.

Then we feel our lungs shaking like drums. The hair on our arms and on the back of our necks stands up and we shake as flights of fighters roar over the hill. They are no more than fifty feet above us. We can feel the heat from the tailpipes, and the orange flames are blinding. The noise is superb. They come three at a time; one wave, two, three, four, five, and six. These are our pilots. The mass of the machinery flying through the air is so great and graceful that we are stunned beyond the noise. We cheer in anger and in satisfaction. It seems the best thing in the world when, as they pass the ridge (How they hug the ground; what superb pilots!) they dip their wings for our sake. They are descending into a thicket of anti-aircraft missiles and radar-directed guns—and they dip their wings for us.

Now we are hot. The married men feel as if rivers are rushing through them, crossing and crashing, for they are angry and full of energy. The sergeant depresses the lever on the microphone. He identifies himself and says, "In the name of God, we want to go in *now*. Damn you if you don't let us go in."

There is hesitation and silence on the other end. "Who is this?" they ask.

"This is Shimon."

More silence, then, "Okay, Shimon. Move! Move!"

The engines start. Now we have our own thunder. It is not even three o'clock. It is the right time; they've caught us at the right time. The soldiers are not slow in mounting the half-tracks. The sound of our roaring engines has magnetized them and they *jump* in. The young drivers race the engines, as they always do.

For a magnificent half minute, we stare into the north light, smiling. The man who tasted the sweet taste of his wife kisses his wrist. The young soldiers are no longer afraid, and the married men are in a perfect sustained fury. Because they love their wives and children, they will not think of them until the battle is over. Now we are soldiers again. The engines are deafening. No longer are we held back. We are shaking; we are crying. Now we stare into the north light, and listen to the explosions below. Now we hear the levers of the gearshifts. Now our drivers exhale and begin to drive. Now we are moving.

A
Vermont
Tale

Many years ago, when I was so young that each snowfall threatened to bar the door and mountain lions came down from the north to howl below my window, my sister and I were sent for an entire frozen January to the house of our grandparents in Vermont. Our mother and father had been instructed by the court in the matter of their difficult and unbecoming love, and that, somehow, was the root of our journey.

After several hours of winding along the great bays of the ice-cluttered Hudson, we arrived in Manhattan only to discover that we had hardly begun. Our father took us to the Oyster Bar, where we tried to eat oysters and could not. Then he found a way to the high glass galleries in Grand Central, where we watched in astonishment as people far below moved in complete silence, smoothly crossing the strong, sad light which descended in wide columns to the floor. We were told that Vermont would be colder than Putnam County, where we lived, the snow deeper, the sky clearer. We were told that we had been there before in winter but did not remember, that our summer image of the house had been snowed in, and that our grandfather had, of all things, snowshoes.

We were placed in the care of a tremendously fat conductor on a green steam-driven train called Star of the

North, which long after darkness had the temerity to
charge out into the black cold, and speed through snow-
covered fields and over bridges at the base of which mur-
derous ice groped and cut. We knew that outside the windows a man without his coat would either find fire or die.
We sensed as well that the warmth in the train and its
bright lights were not natural but, rather, like the balanc-
ing of a sword at the tip of a magician's finger—an
achieved state, from which an overconfident calculation,
a graceless move, an accident of steel might hurl us into
the numbing water of one of the many rivers over which
the conductor had passed so often that he gave it no
thought. We feared many things—especially that our parents would not come back together and that we would
never go home again. And there was the nagging suspicion
that our grandfather had turned into an illogical ogre,
who, for unimaginable reasons, chose to wear shoes made
of snow.

At midnight, the conductor brought us a pewter tureen of black-bean soup. He explained that the kitchen
had just shut down, and that this was the last food until
breakfast. We had had our filet of sole in the dining car,
and were not hungry at all. But the way he bustled about
the soup, and his excitement at having spirited it to us,
created an unforeseen appetite. In company of the steam
whistle and the glittering ice formed against our window,
we finished it and dispatched a box of crackers besides.
My sister was young enough so that the conductor could
take her on his endless lap and show her how to blow
across her spoon to cool the soup. She loved it. And I remember my own fascination with the gold watch chain
which, across his girth, signified the route between Portu-
gal and Hawaii.

All through the night, the Star of the North rushed

on, its whistle gleaming across frost-lined valleys. We were both in the upper bunk. My sister asked if morning would come. I replied that I was sure it would.

"What will it be like?" she said.

"I don't know," I answered, but she was already asleep.

The cold outside was magical, colder than anything we had known.

White River Junction had frozen into place, caught as it crept up the hill. The morning was so bright that it seemed like a dream flooded by spotlights. It was a shock to breathe the cold air, and our grandparents saw at once that we were not warm enough in our camel-colored loden coats.

"Don't you children have Christmas hats?" asked my grandfather.

Not knowing exactly what these were, I kept silent for fear of giving the wrong answer.

"Well," he said quietly, "we're going to have to get you kids Christmas hats and goose vests."

Christmas hats were knit caps of the softest, whitest wool. In a band around the center were ribbons of color representing the spectrum, from a shimmering deep violet to dark orange. Goose vests were quilted down-filled silk. They came to us in wire baskets shooting along a maze of overhead track in a store so vast and full of stuff that it seemed like the world's central repository for things. A distant clerk pulled hard on a hanging lever and there was an explosive report after which the basket careered across the room like a startled pheasant. In the store were high thin windows, through which we saw a perfectly blue sky, parts of the town, an ice-choked river, and brown trees and evergreens on the opposite bank, standing on the hill like a dumbfounded herd. We bought so much in that store that we completely filled the pickup truck with sacks, boxes, packages, bags, and bushel baskets. We bought, among other things, apples, lamb, potatoes, oranges, mint, coffee, wine, sugar, pepper, chocolate, thread, nails, balsa wood, color film, shoe wax, flour, cinnamon, maple sugar, salt fish, matches, toys, and a dozen children's books—good long thick ones with beautiful pictures and heavy fragrant paper.

Then we drove off in the truck. I sat in the middle and my sister was on my grandmother's lap, her little head pointed straight at the faraway white mountains visible through the windshield. I saw my grandmother looking at the way my sister's eyes were focused on the distance; in my grandmother's restrained smile, lit by bright light coming shadowless from the north, was more love than I have ever seen since. They both had blue eyes; and I felt only pain, because I knew that the moment would pass—as it did.

With tire chains singing and the heater blowing, we drove all the way up into Addison County, to the empty quarter, where there are few towns. It seemed odd, after coming all that way, when my grandfather told me that we were close to New York. "The boy doesn't understand," said my grandmother. "We'll have to get a map." Then she looked at me: "You don't understand." Of course, I knew that, especially since I had just heard it declared a minute before. "New York goes all the way up to Canada, and so does Vermont. Massachusetts and Connecticut are in between, but alongside New York. You and Julia came through Connecticut and Massachusetts. But New York was always on your left, to the west."

"Oh," I said.

On a bluff high above a rushing river, we pulled into

a shed at the end of a long snow-covered road. The river forked above my grandparents' land, and came together again south of it. In winter, one could not cross the boiling rapids except by a cable car, which went from the shed to a pine grove behind their barn. The cable car was cream-colored and blue, and had come, we were told, from Switzerland. The two hundred acres were a perfect island.

This island was equally divided into woods, pasture, and lakes. The woods were evergreen, and my grandfather picked up fallen branches whenever he came upon them (for kindling), so that the floor was open and clear, covered only with pine needles and an occasional grouping of ferns. The pines were tall and widely spaced. Horses could gallop through the columned shadows. The chamber formed by these trees extended for acres, in some places growing very dark, and to walk through it was fearsome and delightful. Always, the wind whistled through the trees. If you looked around and saw only this forest, it seemed as if you were underground. But a glance upward showed sky through green.

The pastures were fenced with split rail and barbed wire, covered with deep snow, spread about in patches of five or ten acres in the woods and on the sides of hills. They rolled all over the island and were host to wind and drifts; they were the places to ski or go race the horses on trails that had been packed down by daily use. Half in woods, half in pasture, was the house—white frame with black shutters, many fireplaces, and warm plank floors which gave off resinous squeaks. Between the house and the river was the barn, in which were two horses, a loft of clean hay, a workshop, and a pair of retrievers—one

gold and one black—whose tails were forever waving back
and forth in approval and contentment.

At the island's center were two lakes. One, of about
five acres, lay open to the north wind and was isolated
from the winter sun by a pine-clad rise to its south. This
lake froze so that its surface was as slick as a mirror. When
it was not covered with snow, it was the perfect place to
skate. The second lake was no more than three acres, and
it lay in the lee of the rise, open to the sun. A salt spring
dropped water to it over falls of ten or fifteen feet. It was
bordered by pines and forest-green rocks on the north, and
opened to a pasture below. This lake was nearly hidden,
and it was never completely frozen.

After a few trips in the cable car, we got the provi-
sions and supplies into the house and spent a long time
unpacking and putting away what we had bought. My
grandfather and I took turkeys, hams, chickens, roasts,
and wheels of cheese into a cold smokehouse. When he
lit the fire there, I was poised to run from a great confla-
gration, and was surprised that it crept slowly, with hardly
any flame. That night, we smelled not only sweet fires in
the house but a dark, antique scent from chips smoldering
under hanging meat and fowl.

Our room was in the attic. It had a big window
through which we could see mountain ranges and clouds
beyond the meadows. At night, a vast portion of sky was
visible from our bed. When I opened my eyes after being
asleep, the stars were so ferociously bright that I had to
squint. They were not passive and mute as they sometimes
are, but they shone out and burned like white fire. I have
never fallen asleep without thinking of them. They made
me imagine white lions, perhaps because the phosphorescent burning was like a roar of light. A fireplace was in
the room; a picture of Melville (the handsomest man I

have ever seen, surely not so much for what he looked like
but for what he was); wooden pegs on which to hang our
goose vests and Christmas hats; shelves and shelves of il-
lustrated books. Most remarkably, the ceiling was painted
a deep luminous blue.

As the days became calibrated into wide periods of
light and dark, we lost track even of the weeks, much less
the hours. Later, when I was wounded in war, they shot
me full of morphine. The slow bodiless breathing was just
like the way time passed in that crystalline January.

We were possessed by the flawless isolation and the numbing cold. Perhaps we lost ourselves so easily because of
the exquisite tiredness after so many hours outdoors, or
perhaps because Julia and I had been waiting tensely and
were suddenly freed. In the days, we rode the horses, and
the dogs followed. At first, the four of us went out, with
the children sitting forward on the saddles. Soon, though,
I did my own riding. My grandmother and Julia would
go back into the house and I would mount their horse.
Then my grandfather and I galloped all over the island,
dashing through the pines, crossing meadows, riding hard
to prospects overlooking the thunderous white forks of the
river. Much work was needed just to take care of the
horses, to curry, to shovel, to fork down their hay from
the loft. We split wood and carried it into the house, stock-
ing all the fireplaces every night for at least one good burn.
We baked pies according to a special system, in which my
grandmother made pie for the grownups and we followed
her, step by step, with a children's pie, which, no matter
what we did, always looked like a shanty. My sister kept
the house completely free of dust. It was a game for her,
and she polished everything in sight.

"It's sad," said my grandfather.

"Why?" asked his blue-eyed wife, still strikingly beautiful.

"The child is so upset that she's become obsessed. Today, she was dusting for two hours, telling herself stories and singing. She's afraid to sit still."

"She's as happy as she can be in the circumstances."

"I don't know," he said. "How do you reach a child caught up like that? You can't just talk to her."

"All we have to do is love her, and that's easy."

In late afternoon as it grew dark we would come into the house and read, or be read to, until dinner. After we had cleaned up, we had a fire in the living room and read some more. An old radio brought in a classical station which sounded so far away that it seemed to be Swiss. Sometimes we took walks in the moonlight, and sometimes we stayed out for as long as we could and looked through a telescope at the moon and planets. By about eight, we were always so tired that we hardly moved, and just sat staring at the fire. Then my grandfather would throw on some logs and say, "Enough of this nonsense! Are we sloths? Certainly not. There are things to do. Let's do them."

In a sudden burst of energy, my grandmother would go to the piano, he would return to his book, Julia would pull down the watercolors, the fire would blaze, and I would become hypnotized by Hottentots and Midwestern drainage canals within the dentist-yellow *National Geographic*s. Then we would go to bed, as exhausted as if we had just spent time in a great city at Christmas. Sleep came easily when the nights were clear and the sky pulsed.

But the nights were not always clear. In the middle of January, we had a great blizzard. We could neither ride, nor ski, nor walk for very long with the snowshoes. High drifts made it extremely difficult just to get the wood in.

The sky was gray; my grandfather's bad leg made him limp about; and we all began to grow pale. Instead of putting more logs on the fire and waking up, we let the flame go into coals, and we moved slowly upstairs to sleep. The blizzard lasted for days. We felt as if we were in the Arctic, and we learned to wince slightly at the word "Canada." I wondered if indeed all things came to sad and colorless ends.

Then something happened. One night, when the wind was so fierce that we heard trees crash down in the forest, we were just about to get into bed, and my grandfather had turned out all the lights and was coming up the stairs. From high above in the swirl of raging wind and snow came a frightening, wonderful, mysterious sound.

Neither of the nightingale nor of the wolf but somewhere in between, as meaningful and mournful as a life spent in the most solitary places, strong and yet sad, as clear as cold water and ever so beautiful, it was the cry of the loon. It sounded for all the world like one of Blake's angels, and as it hovered above our house, circling our bed, we thought it was God come to take us. My grandfather rushed to the landing.

"They're back!" he cried.

"It can't be," said my grandmother, looking up. "Not after ten years. They must be others."

"No," he said. "I know them too well."

The sound kept circling and we listened for many minutes with our heads thrown back and our eyes traversing to and fro against the pitch of the roof. Then there was quiet.

"What was it?" I asked, noticing for the first time that my sister had grasped my waist and still held tightly.

"Arctic Loons," he said. "Two Arctic Loons. Isn't it a beautiful sound? I'll tell you about them."

"When?"

"Now," he said, and went to light the fire.

My grandmother dragged in a chair, and she and my grandfather sat facing us. We were propped up in bed, covered by a giant satin goose blanket. It was very late for my sister, and she looked drugged. But she was terrified, and she stared ahead without a blink. She wore a white flannel gown with tiny blue stars all over it. My grandmother rocked back and forth, hardly ever taking her eyes from us. My grandfather leaned forward as if he were about to enter communion with the blazing fire.

Then he turned with startling concentration. My grandfather was six and one-half feet tall and as thin as a switch. He was rocking back and forth, and he mesmerized us as if we were a jury and he a great lawyer of the nineteenth century. The fire roared upward at the stone, diverging into ragged orange tongues. "What is a loon? What is a loon? What is a loon?" he said, so that our mouths dropped open in astonishment.

"You heard it, did you not? Can you tell me that the creature has no soul? Doesn't it sound, in its sad call, like a man? Did they not sound like singers? Remember, first of all, that we have our idea of angels from the birds. For they are gentle and perfect in a way we will never be. For more than a hundred million years they have been soaring. They found the union of peace and ecstasy so long ago that we cannot even imagine the time. But that does not answer your simple question.

"A loon is a bird. Tomorrow, you will see it. It is extremely fine to look at, so sleek and clean of line that it puts an arrow to shame. It is circumpolar, which means that it lives in both the Eastern and the Western hemispheres. It can swim on the water and under it, and it is a strong flier. Tonight we heard two Arctic Loons. When winter comes in the polar regions, they go south. But rarely do they appear on the Atlantic Coast, and when they do they winter on the sea, where the water, though cold, is not frozen, and where there are plenty of fish.

"When I came back from the First War, your grandmother and I bought this place and began to spend the summers here. The house was up, but most of the pasture was not cleared, the barn had yet to be built, and the only way over the river was by a cable ferry on which everything got a thorough wetting. For years, we were here only in the summer, but one winter I came to stay alone.

"It was almost impossible to cross the river on the ferry. Had it capsized into the freezing waters, I would have drowned. The sheriff of the county advised me not to cross, but I did, and soon I was snowed in and everything was completely quiet. In those days, I was trying to write my dissertation. Before you become a professor, you have to write a book which is boring enough so that even you cannot bear to read it over. Once you have done this, you are free to write as you please, but can't. After I had been in the war, it was hard to write such a book because, well, I was so happy just to be alive—so happy that for years afterward I often did crazy things."

My grandmother glanced leftward into the darkness above the roof beams, conveying both skepticism and amusement. But, when she returned her gaze to my grandfather's face, she seemed almost bitter.

"For example," my grandfather continued. "In Cambridge, Harvard students were supposed to be afraid of the town toughs, who always gathered in large groups at street corners. Though I knew my way around (after having been there for ten years), I would sometimes approach such a group and say, 'Which one of you duds knows

enough words to direct me to Kirkland Street?' That, believe me, took courage. And then, once, I stood up in a
crowded lecture and asked the professor: 'What is the dif-
ference between a mailbox and the backside of a hippopot-
amus?' He immediately said, 'I don't know,' to which I
answered that I would be glad to mail his letters for him.
I believe it was the shock of war. I hope it was the shock
of war. It took me a while to straighten out.

"After a few days in the house, struggling to write
my chapters, I grew restless and began to walk around in
the woods. We did not have horses then. I went to the big
lake and found that it had a snowless surface. I skated
there for a week before I went to the little lake, to see if
perhaps I could skate there, too. When I saw that it was
clear of ice, I remembered that it was salty and sheltered.
As I was sitting, skates hung over my shoulder, my face
to the sun, a fleet of birds sailed gracefully from under a
rock ledge to the center of the lake. There were at least
a dozen loons—paired up, healthy, unaware of my presence. I moved back so that they would not see me, and
when I left I resolved to watch them in secret.

"This I did, and soon learned their habits. Early in
the morning, the first flight—as I called it—would take
off from the lake with great effort. It was so hard for them
to get airborne that it seemed as if they would crash
against the opposite shore, but they rose just before the
land and flew southward. This they did two at a time until
about noon, when the first pair returned. The last flight
returned just at darkness. Then they would go up on the
bank and sleep in nests they had made of fern, pine needles, and reeds.

"Though their transition to flight was awkward, they
flew magnificently—as I learned later, up to sixty miles
per hour. Because of their great speed, I was at first unable

to follow them. But one day I was in town and had just stepped out of the post office, when I saw two of them flying by in the same direction as the road. You can imagine the surprise of the sheriff when I jumped into his idling car and ordered him to follow the loons. He did, and we discovered that they fed in a wide section of the river, where there were many fish but where the loons could not have lived because the water ran too fast. I watched them over time and found that they lived in mated pairs, that they kept faith, and that they showed great concern and tenderness for one another. In fact, their loyalty and intimacy were as beautiful to observe as their graceful bodies of brown, white, and gray.

"I soon discovered an attached pair which seemed to be special. Though the female was not as majestic as some, and though she modestly moved about her business and did not lord it over the group as others did, she was extraordinarily beautiful—despite her imperfections, or perhaps because of them. She had a gentleness, a quietness, a tentativeness, which showed how finely she was aware of the sad beauty in the life they lived. You could see the seasons on her face, and that she felt and suffered deeply. Nonetheless, she was a strong and robust flier. This combination intrigued me, this union of gentleness and strength.

"Her mate was full of energy and wounds. Part of his foot was missing. A great gash was cut into his wing. You see, he and others like him had flown into the hunters' guns. Fishermen think that loons steal their catch. This is incorrect, and yet the loons are hunted down time and again, and their number steadily decreases. This may explain why they had chosen a small lake in lieu of an abundant sea.

"Anyway, he was alternately gregarious and reclu-

sive. Sometimes he led or harried the others, and sometimes he would not go near them. For her, this was most
difficult. Loons are good fliers and graceful swimmers.
They can stay under water for several minutes, and they
have been observed to dive as far as two hundred and fifty
feet below the surface. But on land they can hardly move,
because they are, I think, the only bird whose leg is mainly
within the body, so much are they like swimmers. When
moving on land, they waddle and they fall. Many, many
times, he went up onshore and pushed for the woods. I
saw her looking after him. It pained her to see him moving
so awkwardly into the thicket, where perhaps a fox might
get him. It made her feel as if she were not loved. For if
she were, she thought, why would he take such risks? But
he was driven in all directions and frequently made her
feel alone and apart. And yet she loved him, and she loved
him very strongly, despite what appeared to be her reti-
cence.

"They would lie up against one another, have long
conversations in their many voices, circle the lake, and
sometimes put their faces together so that their eyes
touched. The days passed one after another until it became
irredeemably dark. Then, from the north, another group
of loons came winging in and threw the lake into chaos.
They were unattached, and their arrival electrified the others.

"She felt immediately threatened because of his curiosity and the way he had always wandered away. This
frightened her, and she kept to herself, closing off to him.
All *he* knew was that she became colder and colder. He
did not realize that she loved so much that her fear ran
ahead of her, and he began to take up with the group from
the north. He paid much attention to one in particular—a

brilliant female, with whom one day he flew off to the feeding place, where the river was fast and full of fish.

"She was so hurt that she could not even think. And when he returned, enthused and energized, she was hurt all the more. But it would have passed had he not done it again and again, until she was forced to go alone south to the feeding place, and fish alone in front of all while he was occupied with the new one. And she flew back alone, her heart beating against the rhythm of her wings, her eyes nearly blind, for she loved him so much, and he had betrayed her.

"As time passed, the pain was too much for her to bear, and she left. Her departure worked through him like a harrow, and all was changed. As in the classical Greek and Latin romances, he realized what he had done, and, more to the point, how valuable she was and how he loved her, and he was thrashed with remorse. He set out to find her. Despite his skill and experience as a flier and a fighter, it was extremely difficult. She had gone to a lake deep, deep in the wilderness and very far away."

"Baltimore," said my grandmother, startling herself, and then realizing that it was late and that the story would have to continue on the next night. "Besides," she said to my grandfather, "if the blizzard keeps up, you won't be able to take the children to the small lake. They can see the loons the day after tomorrow."

When they had kissed us good night and opened the window enough so that the room began to cool rapidly and hard, dry crystals of snow were blown in only to disappear in the darkness beyond the bed, we were left alone in the light of the fire. Breathing hard, my little sister stared at the flames, her eyes all welled up. It was like a fever night, when there is no relief. In those reddened nights, little children first conjured up the idea of Hell.

I tried, as I always did, to be very grownup. But I really couldn't.

It snowed so hard the next day that the air was like tightly loomed cloth. Drifts covered the porch and reclined against the windows. The house was extremely quiet. We had stayed up late and were tired from days of being trapped inside. My grandfather and grandmother said hardly a word, not even to one another.

When it darkened—and it darkened early—we began to anticipate resumption of the tale as if we were awaiting Christmas morning: the four of us in a small room with a sky-blue ceiling, an enginelike fire steadily cascading like a forge, snow against the window, the goose blanket spread out silky and white like a winter meadow, and the story unraveling in dancing shadows. Before we knew it, the yellow disc in the clock plunged downward and was replaced by a sparkling white moon and stars on a background of blue. The moon had a strange smile, and I thought that he must have been born on that island a long time before, and spent his life in the perfect quiet—season after season, silent snow after silent snow.

My grandfather put two more split logs on the fire in our room, and started once again to tell us about the loons. I looked at the ceiling and imagined them as they had been the night before, poised above us, treading with brown wings on the agitated air.

"He hardly knew what he was in for," said the old man, closing his eyes briefly and then opening them as he began the tale. "He was so good-spirited that he envisioned a fast flight to a lake found out by skill, swooping to reunion, and then beginning where they had left off. But he didn't count on two things. The first was her feeling that she had been horribly betrayed, and the second, and more immediate, was the problem of how to find her.

"He set off, rising into the air with a rush from his wings. He flew for many miles, and after a day he did not see her on any of the lakes beneath. He stayed one night on a large lake where it was cold and there were no living things, but only a whistling mysterious wind. He traversed the dark northern lakes as if they were chambers in a great cavern, always alone, flying through the relentless cold, day after day and week after week, with his eyes sharp and his great strength serving him well, until he had flown enough for several migrations and was nearly beaten. The ice cut him; he was pursued by hungry forest animals; and in all those regions of empty whiteness he never came upon another of his kind."

"How do you know?" I asked. He looked at me imperiously, greatly offended. I began to be frightened of him.

"Because I know," he said, and from then on I did not dare to question him, although I did wonder how he could know such a thing.

"For months, he read the terrain and searched for the proper signs. Then, as he was about to land on one of a chain of lakes, he saw a flight of many loons far off in the distance, disappearing over a hill of bare trees.

"He sprinted toward them. Since he had flown all day, he was lithe and hot, and caught them so quickly that they thought an eagle had flown into their midst. She was there! He spotted her at the edge, in company of several others. He dived at them and drove them off, and then flew level with her, on the same course as the rest but at a distance.

"She would not look at him, and she acted as if he were dead to her. After they landed, she, to his great sadness, went off with another. But he could easily see that she did not love the other. Nor was the other a champion, a strong flier, or wounded by the hunters' guns.

"All his persuasion, his sorrow, meant nothing to her. She seemed determined to spend her life, without feeling, in the presence of strangers. So he left without her. It was painful for him to see her recede into the distance as he flew away.

"Alone on the little lake, he did not know what to do. He had got to know her so well, and come to love her so deeply, that he did not feel that he could ever love another. He began to think of the hunters' guns. It gave him great pleasure to imagine flying against them, even though he would be killed. But he was kept from this by the chance that she would return. He waited. Days passed, months. As the seasons turned and it was winter once again, he realized that he had lost his chance. If at the end of another winter she did not return, he would then set off to seek out the hunters.

"When storms came down from the north in the second winter, he realized that she would not return. For she would by then have been driven south. Nor did the others arrive, and he found himself in sole possession of the lake. He made no more forays into the trees and brush. He stopped singing on clear nights. Until that time, he had sung loudly and beautifully in hope that she would use the sound to guide herself back. On those nights in the fall when the air is refined and clear and the moon beats down by black shadows in a straight white line, he had sung the last out of himself. As winter took hold, he moved in a trance, determined to find the hunters in the spring. Her image so frequently filled the darkness before him that he did not trust his sanity.

"Sensible loons (if there can be such a term) were supposed to get on with work. But he cared little for making himself fat with fish and could not see years ahead of simply eating. The winter closed him in. He would sit in the disheveled nest and stare without feeling as the sun refracted through ice and water. The blue sky seemed to run through his eyes like a brook.

"But one day in early March, when the sun was hot enough to usher out some light green and the blue lakes seemed soft and new, he glanced up at a row of whitened Alpine clouds and saw a speck sailing among them as if in a wide circle. It was a bird, far away, alone in the sky, orienting. And then the bird slid down the sides of the clouds and beat her way around them and fell lower and lower in a great massive glide, swooping up sometimes, turning a little, and finally pointing like an arrow to the lake.

"He trembled from expectation and fear. But he knew her flight. He knew the courage she had always had, despite her frailty, in coursing the clouds. And on that last run, as she came closer and closer, she became an emblem of herself. He sped to the middle of the lake with all the energy he had unwittingly saved. The blood was rushing through him as if he had been flying for a day, and she swooped over his head, turned in the air like an eagle, and landed by him in a crest of white water."

When my grandfather said that, his hands were before him and he sat bolt upright in his chair. My sister closed her eyes and let out a sigh. This, my grandmother liked very much. For the little girl had been tensed and contorted awaiting the outcome. Suddenly, the circling of the loons above the house made perfect sense. It was as if winter were somehow over, though that was far from true.

As my sister slept profoundly, it was my turn to spend

a fever night. Though it was deathly cold, there was enough light to think upon, and I troubled until morning.

Very early, when I could sleep only in fits and starts, I arose and jumped quietly to the floor. Everyone was asleep. It was light, but it still snowed. I put on my clothes and boots and went down the stairs. There was ice on the inside of the windows. Not knowing about condensation, or much else, I thought the ice had come through the glass. Outside, I put on snowshoes and heatedly made my way around the house. I could hear the snow falling. It sounded like a slow and endless fire. I caught whiffs from the smoke shed, and was aware of a vague sweet smell from the house chimneys.

I followed the tops of the fence posts and the straight ribbon between the trees which showed the road. The snowshoes were too big and I tumbled several times into the snow, discovering in both delight and horror that it came up to my chin. But, puffing along the top of the drifts, I finally came to the lake. It was partially covered by ice, on which lay a slope of snow.

Under the rock ledge, a wide space of open water smelled fresh even from a distance. The snow came down in steady lines, but I squinted and made out two gliding gray forms, hardly visible, moving as if in the severest of all mysteries. I dared not approach them, though I could have. They seemed like lions on the plain, or spirits, or frightening angels.

Then I turned at the sound of snowshoes and saw my grandmother coming up the rise to where I stood. When she reached me, she put her hand on my shoulder and looked hard at the loons. She, too, looked sleepless.

"I heard you," she said, "when you left the house. Do you see them?"

For reasons I could not discern, I began to cry. She

dropped to her knees, kneeling on her snowshoes, and took me in her arms. She didn't have to say anything. For I saw that her eyes . . . her eyes, though beautiful and blue, were as cold as ice.

White
Gardens

It was August. In the middle of his eulogy the priest said,
"Now they must leave us, to repose in white gardens," and
then halted in confusion, for he had certainly meant green
gardens. But he was not sure. No one in the overcrowded
church knew what he meant by white gardens instead of
green, but they felt that the mistake was in some way appropriate, and most of them would remember for the rest
of their lives the moment afterward, when he had glanced
at them in alarm and puzzlement.

The stone church in Brooklyn, on one of the long avenues stretching to the sea, was full of firefighters, the press,
uncharacteristically quiet city politicians in tropical suits,
and the wives and eighteen children of the six men who,
in the blink of an eye, had dropped together through the
collapsing roof of a burning building, deep into an
all-consuming firestorm.

Everyone noticed that the wives of the firemen who
had died looked exceptionally beautiful. The young
women—with the golden hair of summer, in dark print
dresses—several of whom carried flowers, and the older,
more matronly women who were less restrained because
they understood better what was to become of them, all
had a frightening, elevated quality which seemed to rule
the parishioners and silence the politicians.

The priest was tumbling over his own words, perhaps because he was young and too moved to be eloquent according to convention. He looked up after a long silence and said, simply, "repose of rivers . . ." They strained to understand, but couldn't, and forgave him immediately. His voice was breaking—not because so many were in the church, for in the raw shadow of the event itself, their numbers were unimpressive. It wasn't that the Mayor was in the crowd: the Mayor had become just a man, and no one felt the power of his office. It may have been the heat. The city had been under siege for a week. Key West humidity and rains had swept across Brooklyn, never-ending, trying to cover it with the sea. The sun was shining now, through a powerful white haze, and the heat inside the church was phenomenal and frightening, ninety-five degrees—like a boiler room. All the seasons have their mystery, and perhaps the mystery of summer is that it overwhelms with easy life, and makes one feel improperly immortal.

One of the wives glanced out a high window and saw white smoke billowing from a chimney. Even in this kind of weather, she thought, they have to turn on the furnaces to make hot water. The smoke rushed past the masonry as if the chimney were the stack of a ship. She had been to a fireman's funeral before, and she knew what it was going to be like when the flag-draped coffin was borne from the church and placed on the bed of a shiny new engine. Hundreds of uniformed men would snap to attention, their blue hats aligning suddenly. Then the procession would flow away like a blue river, and she, the widow (for she was now the widow), would stagger into a waiting black car to follow after it.

She was one of the younger wives, one of those who were filled with restrained motion, one of the ones in a dark print dress with flowers. She was looking to the priest for direction, but he was coming apart, and as he did she could not keep out of her mind the million things she was thinking, the things which came to her for no reason, just the way the priest had said "white gardens," and "repose of rivers." She thought of the barges moving slowly up the Hudson in a tunnel of silver and white haze, and of the wind-polished bridges standing in the summer sun. She thought of the men in the church. She knew them. They were firefighters; they were rough, and they carried with them in the church more ambition, sadness, power, courage, greed, and anger than she cared to think about on this day. But despite their battalion's worth of liveliness and strength, they were drawn to the frail priest whose voice broke every now and then in the presence of the wives and the children and the six coffins.

She thought of Brooklyn, of its vastness, and of the things that were happening in Brooklyn, right then. Even as the men were buried, traffic on the streets and parkways would be thick as blood; a hundred million emotions would pass from soul to soul, into the air, into walls in dark hot rooms, into thin groves of trees in the parks. Even as the men were buried in an emerald field dazzling with row upon row of bone-white gravestones, there would be something of resurrection and life all over Brooklyn. But now it was still, and the priest was lost in a moment during which everyone was brought together, and the suited children and lovely wives learned that there are quiet times when the world is touched, and when that which is truly important arises to claim all allegiances.

"It is bitter," said the priest, finally in control of himself, "bitter that only through windows like these do we see clearly into past and future, that in such scenes we burn through our temporal concerns to see that everything that was, is; and that everything that is, will always be." She looked at him, bending her head slightly and pursing her lips in an expression of love and sadness, and he continued. "For we shall always have green gardens, and we shall always have white gardens, too."

Now they knew what he meant, and it shot like electricity through the six wives, the eighteen children, and the blue river of men.

Palais
de Justice

In a lesser chamber of Suffolk County Courthouse on a day in early August, 1965—the hottest day of the year—a Boston judge slammed down his heavy gavel, and its pistol-like report threw the room into disarray. Within a few minutes, everyone had gone—judge, court reporters, blue-shirted police, and a Portuguese family dressed as if for a wedding to witness the trial of their son. The door was shut. Wood and marble remained at attention in dead silence. For quite a while the room must have been doing whatever rooms do when they are completely empty. Perhaps air currents were stabilizing, coming to a halt, or spiders were beginning to crawl about, up high in the woodwork. The silence was beginning to set when the door opened and the defense attorney re-entered to retrieve some papers. He went to his seat, sat down, and ran his hands over the smooth tabletop—no papers. He glanced at the chairs, and then bent to see under the table—no papers. He touched his nose and looked perplexed. "I know I left them here," he said to the empty courtroom. "I thought I left them here. Memory must be going, oh well."

But his memory was excellent, as it had always been. He enjoyed pretending that in his early sixties he was losing his faculties, and he delighted in the puzzlement of where the papers had gone. The first was an opportunity

for graceful abstention and serene neutrality, the second
a problem designed to fill a former prosecutor's mind as
he made his way out of the courthouse, passing through
a great hall arched like a cathedral and mitered by hot
white shafts of grainy light.

Years before, when he had had his first trial, one
could not see the vault of the roof. It was too high and
dark. But then they had put up a string of opaque lighting
globes, which clung to the paneled arches like risen balloons and lit the curving ceiling.

One day a clerk had been playing a radio so loudly
that it echoed through the building. The Mayor of Boston
appeared unexpectedly and stood in the middle of the
marble floor, emptiness and air rising hundreds of feet
above him. "Turn that radio off!" he screamed, but the
clerk could not hear him. Alone on the floor with a silent
crowd staring from the perimeter, the Mayor turned an-
grily and scanned halls and galleries trying to find direction for his rage, but could not tell from where the sound
came and so pivoted on the smooth stone and filled the
chamber with his voice. "I am your mayor. Turn it off,
do you hear me, damn you to hell. I am your mayor!" The
radio was silenced and all that could be heard was the echo
of the Mayor's voice. The defense attorney had looked up
as if to see its last remnants rising through rafters of daylight, and had seen several birds, flushed from hidden nest-
ing places, coursing to and fro near the ceiling, threading
through the light rays. No one but the defense attorney
saw them or the clerk, a homely, frightened woman who,
when the Mayor had long gone, came out and carefully
peered over a balcony to see where he had stood. It was
then that the defense attorney saw the intricate motif of
the roof—past the homely woman, the birds, and the light.

Now he went from chamber to chamber, and hall to

hall, progressing through layers of rising temperature until he stood on the street in a daze. It was so hot that people moved as if in a baking desert, their expressions as blank and beaten as a Tuareg's mask and impassive eyes. The stonework radiated heat. A view of Charlestown—mountains and forests of red brick, and gray shark-colored warships drawn up row upon row at the Navy Yard—danced in bright waves of air like a mirage. Across the harbor, planes made languid approaches to whitened runways. They glided so slowly it looked as if they were hesitant to come down. Despite the heat there was little haze, even near the sea. A Plains August had grasped New England, and Boston was quiet.

"Good," thought the defense attorney, "there won't be a single soul on the river. I'll have it all to myself, and it'll be as smooth as glass." He had been a great oarsman. Soon it would be half a century of near-silent speed up and down the Charles in thin light racing shells, always alone. The fewer people on the river, the better. He often saw wonderful sights along the banks, even after the new roads and bridges had been built. Somehow, pieces of the countryside held out and the idea of the place stayed much the same, though in form it was a far cry from the hot meadows, dirt roads, and wooden fences he had gazed upon in his best and fastest years. But just days before, he had seen a mother and her infant son sitting on the weir, looking out at the water and at him as he passed. The child was so beautiful as the woman held up his head and pointed his puzzled stare out over river and fields, that the defense attorney had shaken in his boat—having been filled with love for them. Then there were the ducks, who slept standing with heads tucked under their wings. Over fifty years he had learned to imitate them precisely, and often woke them as he passed, oars dipping quietly and

powerfully to speed him by. Invariably, they looked up
to search for another duck.

"You shouldn't be going out today, Professor," said
Pete, who was in charge of the boathouse. "No one's out.
It's too hot."

He was a stocky Dubliner with a dialect strong
enough to make plants green. When he carried one end
of the narrow craft down the sloping dock to the river he
seemed to the defense attorney to resemble the compact
engines which push and pull ships in the Panama Canal.
Usually the oarsman holding the stern was hardly as
graceful or deliberative as Pete, but struggled to avoid getting splinters in his bare feet.

"I haven't seen one boat all of today." Pete looked
at him, waiting for him to give up and go home. The defense attorney knew that Pete wanted to call the Depart-
ment of Athletics and have the boathouse closed at two
so he could go to tend his garden. "Really, not one boat.
You could get heat stroke you know. I saw it in North
Africa during the War—terrible thing, terrible thing. Like
putting salt on a leech."

The defense attorney was about to give in, when
someone else walked up to the log book and signed so pur-
posefully that Pete changed his strategy, saying to both
of them, "If I were you now, I wouldn't stay out too long,
not in this weather."

They went as they did each day to get S-40, the best
of the old boats. It was the last boat Pat Shea had built
for Harvard before he was killed overseas. Though already
a full professor in the Law School and over draft age, the
defense attorney had volunteered, and did not see his wife
or his children for three solid years. When he returned—and those were glorious days when his children
were young and suddenly talking, and his wife more beau-

tiful than she had ever been—he went down to the boat-house and there was S-40, gleaming from disuse. Pat Shea was dead in the Pacific, but his boat was as ready as a Thoroughbred in the paddock. For twenty years the defense attorney had rowed loyally in S-40, preferring it to the new boats of unpronounceably named res-ins—computer designed, from wind tunnels, with riggers lighter than air and self-lubricating ball bearings on the sliding seat, where S-40 had seasoned into a dark blood color, and the defense attorney knew its every whim.

As they carried it from the shadows into blinding light, the defense attorney noticed the other sculler. He could not have been much over twenty, but was so large that he made the two older men feel diminutive. He was lean, muscled, and thick at the neck and shoulders. His face was pitted beneath a dark tan, and his hair long and tied up on his head in an Iroquois topknot. He looked like a Spartan with hair coiled before battle, and was ugly and savage in his stance. Nevertheless, the defense attorney, fond of his students and of his son who had just passed that age, smiled as he passed. He received as recompense a sneer of contempt, and he heard the words "old man" spoken with astonishing hatred.

"Who the hell is that?" asked the defense attorney of Pete as they set S-40 down on the lakelike water.

"I don't know. I never seen him before, and I don't like the looks of him. He brought his own boat, too, one of those new ones. He wants me to help him bring it down. Of course I'll have to. I'll take me time, and you can get a good head start so's you'll be alone up river," said Pete, knowing that informal races were common, and that if two boats pulled up even it nearly always became a con-test. He wanted to spare the defense attorney the humilia-tion of being beaten by the unpleasant young man who

had meanwhile disappeared into the darkness of the boat-
house.

As S-40 pulled out and made slowly for the Anderson
Bridge, the young man, whom the defense attorney had
already christened "the barbarian," walked down the
ramp, with his boat across his shoulders. Even from 100
feet out the defense attorney heard Pete say, "You didn't
have to do that. I would have helped you." No matter,
thought the defense attorney, by the time he gets it in the
water, places his oars, and fine tunes all his alloy locks and
stretchers, I'll be at the Eliot Bridge and in open water
with a nice distance between us. He had no desire to race,
because he knew that although he could not beat a young
athlete in a boat half as light as S-40, he would try his best
to do so. On such a hot day, racing was out of the question.
In fact, he resolved to let the young man pass should he
be good enough to catch up. For it was better to be humili-
ated and alive than dead at the finish line. He cannot possibly humiliate me anyway, he thought. A young man in
a new-style boat will obviously do better than a man three
times his age in a wood shell. But, he thought, this boat
and I know the river. I have a good lead. I can pace myself
as I watch him, and what I do not have in strength I may
very well possess in concentration and skill.

And so he started at a good pace, sweeping across
glass-faced waters in the large swelling of the stream just
north of the Anderson Bridge, gauging his speed expertly
from the passage of round turbulent spots where the oars
had been, and sensing on the periphery of vision the me-
tered transit of tall ranks of sycamores on the Cambridge
side. He was the only man on the river, which was glossy
and green with a thick tide of beadlike algae. Always
driven to the river by great heat, dogs loped along with
the gait of trained horses, splashing up a wave as they ran

free in the shallows. S-40 had taut blue canvas decking, and oars of lacquered yellow wood with black and white blades. The riggers were silver-colored, an alloy modification, and the only thing modern about the boat. The defense attorney was lean and tanned, with short white hair. His face was kind and quiet, and though small in stature, he was very strong, and looked impressive in his starched white rowing shorts. The blue decking shone against the green water as in a filtered photograph of a sailing regatta.

It seemed to him that the lonely condition upon the river was a true condition. Though he had had a lot of love in his life, he knew from innumerable losses and separations that one stands alone or not at all. And yet, he had sought the love of women and the friendship of men as if he were a dog rasping through the bushes in search of birds or game. Women were for him so lovely and central to all he found important that their absence, as in the war, was the stiffest sentence he could imagine, and he pictured hell as being completely without them—although from experience he knew that they must have filled a wing or two there to the brim. Often, as he rowed, he slackened to think of the grace and beauty of girls and women he had known or loved. He remembered how sometime in the middle Twenties, when he was courting his wife, he had passed a great bed of water lilies in the wide bay before Watertown. He grasped one for her as he glided by, and put it in the front of the boat. But when he reached the dock the flower had wilted and died. The next day he stopped his light craft and pulled deep down on a long supple stem. Then he tied it to the riggers and rowed back with the lily dangling in the water so that he was able to preserve it, a justly appreciated rare flower. But people did not "court" anymore.

He resumed his pace, even though, without straining,

he was as dripping wet as if he had been in a sauna for five minutes. Rounding the bend before the Eliot Bridge, he saw the young man in his new-style boat, making excellent speed toward him. He had intended to go beyond the Eliot, Arsenal Street, and North Beacon bridges to the bay where the lilies still grew, where it was easy to turn (although he could turn in place) and then to come back. All told, it was a course of six miles. It would not pay to go fast over that distance in such killing heat. If they were to race, the finish would have to be the last bridge out. By the time he passed under the Eliot Bridge, with two more bridges to go, the young man had closed to within a few hundred yards.

His resolutions fell away as if they were light November ice easy to break with oars and prow. Almost automatically, he quickened his pace to that of the young man, who, after a furious initial sprint, had been forced to slow somewhat and retrieve his breath. The defense attorney knew that once he had it he would again pour on speed in the excessive way youth allowed, and so the defense attorney husbanded his strength, going as fast as his opponent but with the greatest possible economy. This he achieved by relaxing, saying to himself, "Easy. Easy. The fight is yet to come. Easy now, easy."

Though the young athlete was a hundred yards downriver the defense attorney could see dark lines of sweat in his knotted hair, and could hear heavy breathing. "I'm a fool," he said, "for racing in this heat. It's over 100 degrees. I have nothing to prove. I'll let him pass, and I'll let him sneer. I don't care. My wisdom is far more powerful than his muscular energy." And yet, his limbs automatically kept up the pace, draining him of water, causing salt to burn his eyes. He simply could not stop.

He remembered Cavafy's *Waiting for the Barbarians,*

which he—in a clearly Western way—had originally assumed to be a lament. Upon reading it he discovered that
the poet shared in the confusion, for it was indeed a lament, that the barbarians were not still on their way. But
for the defense attorney this was unthinkable, for he
dearly loved the West and had never thought that to con-
stitute itself it required the expectation of a golden horde.
And he believed that if one man were to remain strong
and upholding, if just one man were not to wilt, then the
light he saw and loved could never be destroyed, despite
the barbarism of the war, of soulless materialism, of the
self-righteous students who thought to remake this intricate and marvelously fashioned world with one blink of
an untutored eye. If a man can be said to grit his teeth
over a span of years, then the defense attorney had done
just this, knowing that it would both pass and come again,
as had the First War, and the Second, in which he had
learned the great lessons of his life, in which he had been
broken and battered repeatedly—only to rise up again.

He did not want to concede the minor victory of a
river race on a hot day in August, not even that, not even
such a small thing as that to yet another wave of ignorance
and violence. He started with rage in remembering the
sneer. Contempt meant an attack against perceived weakness, and did not weakness merit compassion? If this barbarian had thought him weak, he was up against the gates
of a city he did not know, a stone-built city of towers and
citadels. The defense attorney increased the rapidity of his
stroke to meet his opponent's ominously growing speed.

The young man was gaining, but by very small incre-
ments. Were the defense attorney to have kept up his pace
he would have reached the North Beacon Street Bridge
first, even if only by a few feet. But two things were wrong.
First, such a close margin afforded no recourse in a final

sprint. Because of the unpredictability of the young man's capacities, the defense attorney was forced to build an early lead, which would as well demoralize his rival. Second, not even halfway to the finish, he was beginning to go under. Already breathing extremely hard, he could feel his heart in his chest as if it were a fist pounding on a door.

He was lucky, because he knew the river so well that he had no need of turning to see where he was headed. So precise had the fifty years rendered his navigational sense that he did not even look when he approached bridges, and shot through the arches at full speed always right in the center. However, the young man had to turn for guidance every minute or so to make sure he was not straying from a straight course—which would have meant defeat. That he had to turn was another advantage for the defense attorney, for the young man not only broke his rhythm and sometimes lost his stroke or made a weak stroke when doing so, but he was also forced to observe his adversary still in the lead. If the defense attorney saw the leather thong in the young man's haircomb begin to dip, and saw the muscles in his back uplift a bit, making a slightly different shadow, he knew he was about to turn. This caused the defense attorney to assume an expression of ease and relaxation, as if he were not even racing, and to make sure that his strokes were deep, perfect, and classically executed. He had been in many contests, both ahead and behind.

Though it was a full-blooded race, he realized that he was going no more than half the sustained speed of which he normally was capable. Like a cargo of stone, the heat dragged all movement into viscous slow motion. Time was caught in its own runners, and its elements repeated. Two dogs at the riverside were fighting over a dead carp lapping in the green water. He saw them clash at the

neck. Later, when he looked back, he saw the same scene
again. Perhaps because of the blood and the heat and the
mist in front of his eyes, the salt-stung world seemed to
unpiece in complex dissolution. There was a pattern which
the darkness and the immediacy of the race made him unable to decipher. Intensified summer colors drifted one
into the other without regard to form, and the laziness was
shattered only when a bright white gull, sliding down the
air, passed before his sight in a heartening straight line.

   Though he felt almost ready to die and thought that
he might, the defense attorney decided to implement his
final strategy. About a mile was left. They were nearing
the Arsenal Street Bridge. Here the river's high walls and
banks stopped the wind, and the waters were always
smooth. With no breeze whatsoever, it was all the hotter.
In this quiet stretch races were won or lost. A completely
tranquil surface allowed a burst of energy after the slight
rest it provided. Usually a racer determined to begin his
build-up just at the bridge. Two boats could not clear the
northern arch simultaneously. Thus the rear boat had no
hope of passing and usually resolved upon commencement
of its grand effort after the natural delineation of the
bridge. Knowing it could not be passed, the lead boat
rested to get strength before the final stretch. But the defense attorney knew that his position was in great danger.
A few hundred yards from the bridge, he was only two
or three boatlengths ahead. He could see the young man,
glistening and red, breathing as if struggling for life. But
his deep breathing had not the patina of weakness the defense attorney sensed in his own. He was certain to maintain his lead to the bridge, though, and beyond it for perhaps a quarter of a mile. But he knew that then the
superior strength of the younger man would finally put
the lighter boat ahead. If it were to be a contest of endur-

ance, steady and torturesome as it had been, he knew he
would not win.

But he had an idea. He would try to demoralize the
young man. He would begin his sprint even before the Arsenal Street Bridge, with the benefit of the smooth water
and the lead-in of the arch. What he did was to mark out
in his mind a closer finish which he made his
goal—knowing that there he would have to stop, a good
half mile before the last bridge. But with luck the shocking
lead so far in advance of all expectations would convince
the struggling young man to surrender to his own exhaustion. An experienced man would guess the stratagem. A
younger man might, and might not. If he did, he would
maintain an even pace and eventually pass the defense attorney dead in the water a good distance before the finish
line.

A hundred yards before the Arsenal Street Bridge,
the defense attorney began his massive strokes. One after
another, they were in clear defiance of the heat and his
age. He began to increase his lead. When he passed
through the dark shadow of the bridge, he was already
five boatlengths ahead. He heard the echo of his heart
from the cool concrete, for it was a hollow chamber. Back
in bright light, clubbed by the sun, he went even faster.
The young man had to turn every few seconds to guide
himself through the arch. When he did so he lost much
time in weak strokes, adjustments to course, and breaking
rhythm. But far more important was what he saw ahead.
The old man had begun a powerful sprint, as if up to that
point he had only been warming up.

Three quarters of a mile before the finish the defense
attorney was going full blast. From a distance he looked
composed and unruffled, because all his strength was perfectly channeled. Because of this the young man's stroke

shattered in panic. The defense attorney beat toward his secret finish, breathing as though he were a woman lost deep in love. The breaths were loud and desperate, abandoned and raw, as if of birth or a struggle not to die. He was ten boatlengths ahead, and nearing his finish.

He had not time to think of what he had endured in his life, of the loss which had battered him, and beaten him, and reduced him at times to nothing but a shadow of a man. He did not think of the men he had seen killed in war, whose screams were loud enough to echo in his dreams decades after. He did not think of the strength it had taken to love when not loved, to raise faltering children in the world, to see his parents and his friends die and fall away. He did not think of things he had seen as the century moved on, nor of how he had risen each time to survive in the palace of the world by a good and just fight, by luck, by means he sometimes did not understand. He simply beat the water with his long oars, and propelled himself ahead. One more stroke, he said, and another, and another. He was almost at his end.

He looked back, and a beautiful sight came to his eyes. The young man was bent over and gliding. His oars no longer moved but only brushed the top of the water. Then he began to work his port oar and turn around, for he had given up. He vanished through the bridge.

The defense attorney was alone on the river, in a thickly wooded green stretch full of bent willows. It was so hot that for a moment he forgot exactly who he was or where he was. He rowed slowly to the last bridge. There he rested in the cool shadow of a great and peaceful arch.

A Room of
Frail Dancers

His brigade approached Beersheva in hundreds of trucks crowded in knots on the pale desert road, surging ahead when it put the curves and narrow bridges behind. They arrived at dawn, angry and out of temper. It had taken several weeks to hold the fall, and when they had gotten the upper hand and crossed the canal to take apart the Egyptian Army in the old fierce fashion, they had been forced to stop. Many had died. Many had fought oblivious to danger and death because they were angry and lost.

At sunrise, people came out on their balconies to see the brigade roll in. They stood silently as the thousands passed in a long column. The soldiers were sunburnt and unshaven and their eyes sparkled starlike from dark jagged faces. Some had bandages or slings, and to a man they were armed with submachine guns or automatic rifles, with so many different shining bandoliers of shells that they looked like tigers being carried down the road in drab diesel trucks. They had been riding for several days and were lean and hard from weeks of fighting. They were alive. They returned silent glances to the nightgowned women and the old men on the balconies, glances which told far more than the dead telegraphy which had flooded back over the wires.

The trucks discharged at the station, where, beyond

the platform, a train was steaming and trembling in the white morning sun—wet and cool on its western side, dry and already hot on the eastern side. Then they grouped interminably in lines, to which they were fully accustomed. They surrendered weapons to sullen armorers who cursed because they knew that they would be a month at cleaning. They gave over belts and pouches, helmets, canteens, shovels, and kits, to the back of unmanned trucks into which canvas flew like locusts. At a toss, they were reduced to their black boots and khakis, papers, private weapons, and silver neck chains with the perforated dead tags—one to stay with the body, another to be nailed on the coffin. At card tables set up on the sand near the tracks they were demobilized with a thudding stamp on their blue booklets. Little was said, for they had been without sleep and were worn down.

The train filled slowly. Climbing past its shadowed underbelly, they walked through to semi-compartments with yet another view of desert light and silent sky—a shimmering lamination of beige, blue, and white. In the distance, Bedouins moved a herd of goats—a black mark crawling across faceted hills. Farther still, a frail single-engined observation plane rocked in a straight line across the clear air, heading for an airfield or perhaps away from one.

Rieser's Christian wife had left him (his own fault) and untreatable and progressively worse seizures had driven him back after many years into an army he had once longed to escape, into a war placed as if by design to complement an indifference to death. He felt the deadening of all lively things. Better, he thought, to perish in any kind of affirmation or action, than just to expire. So, he had been content in battle. A casual run across the field of an aerial attack had gotten him between hammered

lines of strafing to an anti-aircraft machine gun, but the
plane passed over the horizon. As if he had been walking
during a break in maneuvers, he had not even bent his
shoulders—and all the time, thunder above and orange
fire from screaming tailpipes. In an attack against two
panicked straggling tanks, he stayed in the open between
them as they turned in the sand, throwing up dust like
twirling gray skirts. As if demonstrating—though even in
demonstrations, they were afraid—he threw grenades at
the tanks, crippling one by breaking up the tread. He
waited for a line of machine gun fire to cut him in two.
The cautious, who were forever hugging a ridge of earth,
were blown to pieces. He was not touched.

Alive in the desert he remembered high lakes and
pines, and delicate singing in an airy church, by which he
was moved to trembling but which he could not accept.
His wife was a beautiful woman with a face like the purest
face of a Renaissance painting. The frailty and mortality
of her features linked her to a high and dominant tradi-
tion. In this little country, they did not know the vast plain
upon which the world was built.

"Chiaro . . . chiaro . . . chiaro," he had once heard
with her in Milan, thinking that in the net of the singing
and in the lilting doubling Italian there was civility and
clarity. He recognized that much would have to be taken
in, cities and words and endless shapes, words like "soldi,"
"chiaro," "incesso," and the understanding behind them.
If he could last until he was old, then perhaps one sweet
line of the music would be totally understood, and the delicate web untangled.

The women's high voices had left him silent and full
of love in a hall swamped with blackness except for a golden quarter of stage. His wife was beside him. He had
wanted to tell her that he did not know how to love her,

that there were walls she could not see, that he was struggling.

The train began to move through the morning, headed as far north as Nahariya, city of the river. Most would get off at Tel Aviv and along the coast. From Haifa, a white ship would carry him to the winter cities of Europe, to Paris—snow, muffled traffic, getting out of a taxi at Villa Mozart and running through the cold to a firelit room full of good friends, or had they moved?

As they crossed the yellow desert a cold light flooded his section. Rieser was one of six soldiers. The light was fine, silver, and clear. Their black eyes sparkled half in shade; their beards were rough and a few days old; they were hard and hollow. One took out a radio and switched it on, skipping to the American station from which came a song: "I'm going uptown to Harlem . . . if the taxi won't take me, I'll catch a train, I'll go underground, I'll get there just the same . . . 125th Street, here I come, get ready for me, 'cause I'm gonna have some fun."

"What does it mean?" asked one of the soldiers.

Rieser offered a translation into Hebrew.

"Under the ground?"

He explained the subway but was interrupted as the soldier held up an orange: "What do you call this?"

"Orange."

The soldier peeled it. It was like watching a primitive man, for he was a young boy and the war had passed by him as if it were a party. "What do you call *this?*"

"Peel," he said, expecting the soldier's reaction, which was to explode into laughter—teeth bared, the pits in his mouth flying to the floor as he choked. The other soldiers, too, laughed, and so did he, since *peel* in Hebrew is the word for elephant.

"I don't believe you."

"It's true," he said, holding up a piece of peel, *"peel."*
Again there was laughter, so much that others were at-
tracted from beyond the partitions. Some laughed so hard
that they fell to the floor and had tears in their eyes. The
train shook, and as it picked up speed they became
charged and excited.

Tel Aviv appeared, spread out flat, white, and green.
The people thought that times were tough, but what a lux-
ury, Tel Aviv, a city of sex and palm-lined streets. They
thought times were bad because prices in the supermarket
had doubled. And what if they had tripled, quadrupled?
If a watch cost 400 pounds, or 800, or 1,000, what differ-
ence did it make? This is why the soldiers laughed so hard.
Their friends had had their heads severed from their bodies. The blood looked as if it were three inches thick on
the ground in pools that quickly hardened. Many were in-
cinerated in tanks, and the smell of seared flesh sometimes
spread for miles. And yet, they had come through, on their
train from the south.

They felt invulnerable, and saw themselves walking
amid the dead as if in a dream. One pass of a screaming
jet with its guns pounding like jackhammers had lightened
them forever. Nothing was to be feared. The planes and
artillery were so much louder than the fastest express, that
the noise in the desert had made the dry passes and undu-
lating rills sound like the inside of a great factory.

At about noon they approached Tel Aviv, running
fast and easy through young orange groves. Plenty of blue
air came in the open window as a thick forest of shiny
green went by, winding, receding, charging full up at them
until some soldiers leaned out and returned with fists full
of broken leaves which filled the car with their fragrance.
Occasionally, a helicopter or a fighter would make a line
across their path. They hardly noticed. A few more hours

until Haifa, a few days going from office to office for clearance, and then he would board a ship for Marseilles. As they left the orange groves, he thought that at least he would live well and for a long time, because he had no desire whatsoever to do either.

Despite his health, there was a flaw. He was often seized and thrown down in dangerous convulsions. These seizures seemed like the country itself, out of control, a shadow play moving according to remote unchallengeable will. The great battles and a lifetime of preparation for them were like the interior of an oratorio. To a man, they felt utterly directed, seized, feebly twitching on a complex stage divided by days of sun and nights under the moon. Fighting in the desert, Rieser had felt entirely beholden. Fighting in the desert, he had finally understood the sad attenuated glances in Renaissance paintings, a meekness and resignation oppressed by full and radiant glory. Once, far away, he had seen an endless column of tanks moving in rays of sun, and their dust cloud had risen like the voices of a choir.

Tel Aviv, the central terminus. Passengers must traverse the length of the city to change trains from South to North Station. It was pleasant to walk the quiet streets, abandoned at noon except for returning soldiers, and he swung toward the sea on Allenby Road, for lunch. The whores were out early to catch soldiers, but the soldiers were not biting. He passed a row of elevated bosoms, stretched satin, and glances like whiskey tossed on hot coals, and went into an eating place where a sizzling rack of lamb turned above a white fire.

He didn't say what he wanted, but, instead, asked the proprietor where he had been in the war.

"In Sinai. Chinese Farm."

"Bad, huh."

"Not so bad, but terrible," the man answered, slicing off a piece of roast meat and offering it to his patron. "On me. You want soda?"

He remembered that he had not eaten since there had been an endlessly high black sky wounded by the scattered broken points of stars. The lamb was good, with a salad, a slice of lemon, and a cold soda. When he left the restaurant, he passed the whores again, dark of skin and painted in sharp angles with the deep colors of the Middle East, colors which lasted through the heat of day, as if fished from cool earthen urns. The line of one girl's eyebrows traveled so far down her cheeks that she looked like a Kabuki actor.

Past villas and industry, ranks of palm and eucalyptus, stagnant canals, whirling hot seascapes, a wildfire sun, and short breathless fields compressed between railroad and sea, he traveled throughout the afternoon to Haifa, the castled port city which ascends a steep mountainside to a crest of dark blue pine.

At one time he and his wife had been thoroughly excited by form, whether of dancers, a painting, the sweep of a sentence, or the slope of a roof. The transportation of clouds across stars, flying over lake country, lace, brought from them an upwelling and sympathy so that they felt like eagles in a chase, skidding from one image to another across patterns and tatters—if not in satisfaction, then in astonishment. Gunning up the rails to Haifa with light reflecting murderously off the sea and the world washed out and white, he absorbed intricacies of form without interest. Wheels on the rails sounded so much like machine guns that he could smell gunpowder. He could make of the ruined villages, the beaches, and the heather-covered hills a construction both wondrous and cold. The spangling sun could not have been more detached.

Calm and quiet, he decided that his love had somehow turned to hate, that his openness had been abused by his own corruption, that the cities were merely complex and no longer magical. The trick of form was in the cold eye after all—how hard he had once fought against that pronouncement, and with what love.

He loved Haifa, into which he rode as evening was about to descend. When he left the train, he had an alert, excited demeanor, a heightened aura which often presaged a bad fall. It was the beginning of November, autumn, a beautiful season filled with passion. Like Mexico in the fall, or any hot dusty place where heat dominates and suddenly the weather becomes mild and clear, Haifa in November was reasoned and bright. He went to a hotel and got a room. The window of the shower looked out on a harbor of lighted ships. When he was clean and had shaved, he put on his pistol (for fear of leaving it in the room) and, still a soldier until the next day when he would turn in his blue book, he went out to walk in the evening. Haifa was very calm, as if it were in the hills of Switzerland or war had never been invented. It was lucid, as if there had been peace for hundreds of years and the populace had only to busy itself with love affairs and the arts.

The war brought out the best, in certain acts of courage and recognition: and the worst, in cowardice and brutality. It did to soldiers far more than kill and maim them: it opened them to a terrible truth against which they had no power. By and large they would rebound, but some had to be left behind. He walked up the side of Mt. Carmel and wound in and among the streets of the Baha'i Gardens, where he looked down to see his ship standing in the harbor. Its tiered superstructure was lit for port. It glowed in darkness like an ice sculpture and soon would take him to a range of entrancing cities. But Haifa, a city of ease and high beauty, was right there. If he could not make his mark from the hills of Haifa and rest content in its gardens of blue-green pine, all the mild art of Europe would hold him no more.

Thinking of how far he had come and how much he had lasted, he felt a surge of courage and determination. The higher he climbed on the eucalyptus-covered hill, the more his past informed his resolution. Climbing upward, he saw a navy yard in snow that fell in chains—a soft hiss at black water, a soundless landing on the whitened ground. He saw himself as an adolescent—crippled with passion, confused, and confident. Those winters of ivory made him smile.

Near the top of the mountain Rieser came upon a hall of dancers, a night class of ballet in a stone building with a red tiled roof. French doors were thrown open to the harbor and back on the hill, from which he could see straight through the hall down to the lights of the ships. The balconies were entangled with flowers. Even in moonlight, he saw that the flowers were red. Inside, a floor of yellowed wood trembled as the dancers leapt and bent to signals of the music. They were all girls just too young to be in the army, and their mistress was herself no more than forty. She carried a baton, which she would sometimes rap sharply on the floor, causing her charges to realign and correct faulty maneuvers. The explosive rap of her baton set them up again and again in rows of violet and blue—the colors of their tights. They stretched tensely, moving about the floor in the grace of dancing, figures of imperfection in constant striving. They crossed in rows and returned with arms high. The watery harbor glinted below them and through the tangle of their limbs. In the transoms, stars shone. The mistress was enraged and encouraging, the girls afraid with expectant eyes, and they sometimes smiled in response to her approval. They danced well and seemed tireless, springing back, losing themselves between the freedom of the music and the discipline of their craft until they seemed almost to cry out in their motion. And their faces had a quickness which struck him. Likened to sound, it seemed as if they had the purity of a horn. And yet he felt that it was purposeless.

He moved to a grove of pine through which a night wind passed. He knew this group of trees, for in the daytime once he had gone there to sleep. When he had opened his eyes, he had breathed in the thin air and a resinous billow was all about him—blue sky like a soft hand at his head.

The ballet class rested. A girl in mauve-colored tights, with a shock of golden hair tied back by a dark velvet ribbon, went to the window to look inward at the hill. Most of the girls stared out at the harbor. Some continued their arches and sweeps in front of mirrors or at the center of the floor. The girl who looked inward was only seventeen. She glanced at the dark wall of pines, and saw a strange sight. A soldier walked slowly into the black, a pistol in his hand. He then disappeared as if into clouds of darkness. She looked up at real moonlit clouds passing over the mountain, and then quickly turned, as if to attention, at the persuasive rap of her mistress's baton. But in the room of frail dancers, the mistress was nowhere to be seen.

La Volpaia

Because there was little that Giuliano Debernardi, with his rigorous high education and his acceptance in ruling circles, could ever bring himself to say to a priest, he looked away in contempt when a small ancient cleric entered his compartment while the train was halted, steaming, before its northward passage through the Alps to Germany. But he was severely startled when the priest slammed a bottle of red wine down on the little folding table, and said, "Who are you that turns his head when a man of the cloth comes in?"

"I beg your pardon."

"You heard me. I'm eighty-six years old and I know I'm going to Heaven. I don't mince words, especially with young intellectuals who imagine that their birth, position, or knowledge make them better than old men who are priests in unknown mountain towns." He spoke in a hoarse, energetic voice, breathing hard and heavy after each declaration. Giuliano Debernardi was indeed a fop, but not a fool. In a show of courage and precision, he held to the position the priest had accurately divined.

"At your age, you should be a Cardinal. Why not the principal in a great academy? You are obviously a failure, and you are aggressive to boot. But I am more aggressive."

The priest threw the bottle at him. It nearly struck

him in his sternum. "Here, open this. It's too difficult for me. I could have been a Cardinal. I could have risen very far in those directions. I chose not to. It was a decision of strength based on a momentous discovery. Give me the wine. Give it. Give it! I can see that you are lost in your own petty concerns. What are your small fears?"

"I am afraid that my German is not good enough," Giuliano Debernardi said quite bluntly.

"Oh? Do you have a German?"

"Please. I am going to Berlin to work for *Zeitschrift für Sozialwissenschaft.* I will have to write in German. I told them I was fluent. They believed me. I am not fluent."

"That's nothing."

"I don't think it's nothing!"

"You have ignored the compression of the world for foolish concerns such as that. And it shows on your face," he added quickly.

"I have ignored the what? What nonsense. I am part of the world. I see things quite deeply. Don't think that I am superficial just because I don't see with your two eyes. I have my own, you know." He leaned over the table and said, quite fiercely, "A stupid assumption, from a provincial priest."

"You think so?"

"Yes. I do." This priest, thought Giuliano Debernardi, is one of those men who are lacking in power, one of those who cannot act decisively, or bring their wills to bear on others. The train began its climb into the snow-covered mountains.

The priest gestured out the window. He seemed hopelessly behind in the competition with Guiliano Debernardi, who began to pity him.

"Look. What do you see?"

"Nothing."

"Nothing! In that instant in which you saw nothing, I saw enough to speak about for a month. Do you remember what we passed? It was a view across a street in a little town near Feltre. In that blink of an eye were a hundred thousand things."

"I saw nothing unusual—just some people walking, the mountains beyond, a wagon or two, an iron fence, I don't know."

"Did you see Emiglia pass?"

"I don't know who Emiglia is."

"In black, near the lip of the gorge. She is a widow. From the way she walked and held herself, you could extract certain details. In that one frame from which you took nothing, Emiglia walked by."

"What of it? There are widows all over Italy. Here, they go by the thousands. I suppose, since the earthquake, years ago."

"No. The young ones have remarried. Others have affairs, taking a man to bed, drawing from him guilty pleasure."

"How do you know?"

"I have sinned."

"I am not impressed."

"I did not do it," said the priest, with a smile, "to impress you."

"Doesn't this Emiglia have affairs, and take men to bed?"

"No, not Emiglia. It is a case somewhat beyond your wisdom—despite your tailored suit and your splendid briefcase. You did not even *see* her walking by the lip of the gorge, that I know. I did not become a Cardinal because . . ."

"Because you like to drink wine."

"What do you know. Cardinals drink as if they were made of sponge. I did not become a Cardinal because . . . it was too thick near Feltre. There was too much. When you encompass affairs, and rule over things, you cannot even start the task.

"Take Emiglia. To you, she was just a flash of black. You did not even see her. She has no affairs. Her husband and six miners rode every day a mile into the mountain, through a tunnel, on bicycles.

"Their way was lit with miner's lamps, and the air was thin and cold. At the tunnel's end, they rose two thousand feet into the heart of the peak. There, they dug silver, under summit ice. With the earthquake, the town was leveled and no one thought of the miners. The mile-long tunnel was shut forever, trapping them in the high chamber." He indicated the enormous mountain, standing astride the rest of the world.

"It isn't that the mountain rides above the town . . . no . . . but," he said slowly, ". . . *their futile movements within the chamber, for time unspecified.* It is difficult to be a young man who has lied to his employer. It is difficult to be an old man who each day just begins to see within an ever-expanding complexity rooted in simple things. It is difficult to be Emiglia, walking by the gorge alone. But none of these things is as difficult, you see, as trying to *draw air through the rock.*"

The train dashed into a tunnel. In the darkness, Giuliano Debernardi struggled in panic to loosen his collar. He felt that there was no air. He could not breathe.

The priest was laughing. For there was, of course, no Emiglia, and his timing had been just right.

Tamar

Before the War, in London, I was trying to arrange a system whereby the Jews of Germany and Austria could sell their paintings and other works of art without depressing demand. It was very serious business, for our primary aim was to require that twenty-five percent of each sale go into an escape fund to provide transport for those who could not make it on their own. We thought that we could exact this price if we managed to keep market values steady. But all of Europe was on edge about the political situation, and no one was in the mood to buy anything. And then, after *Kristallnacht,* every Jew in Germany came forward, wanting to sell precious objects.

At the time of our greatest hope, my job was to set up fronts for selling what we expected would be a flood of art coming in from Middle Europe. If it had appeared that English collectors were opening their storerooms to take advantage of a favorable market, the excitement might well have pushed values upward. So we tried to get the cooperation of those prominent collectors who had the foresight to see what was about to happen on the Continent and were in sympathy with our cause. Excepting a very few, these were Jews. The others simply were not interested, and, anyway, we did not want to divulge the plan in too many places.

Soon I found myself deeply involved in the high society of Jews in London and in their great houses throughout the countryside. My conviction was then, as it is now, that it is not possible for Jews to be in "society" but that their efforts to be so are (except when immoderate or in bad taste) courageous, for the mechanisms of high social status are encouragements of vulnerability, safe only for those who can afford to lose themselves in pursuits superficial and deep and not fear that their fundamental positions will drop out from under them as a result of their inattention. My attitude toward the Jewish peers and the Jewish upper class in general was mixed, and had complex roots. I admired their bravery while occasionally chafing at their blindness. I knew that, in spite of their learning and culture, they were isolated in such a way as to make me—a young man of thirty-two—far better a judge of certain things than were they. I had been in the ghetto in Warsaw not a month before, and the people there had confided to me that they felt the end was near. They said, "Tell them, in England, that in Poland they are killing Jews." I had been in Berlin, Munich, Vienna, and Prague. I had passed through Jewish villages from Riga to Bucharest, where I had seen a temple about to fall. How misty and beautiful it was, that autumn. I cannot describe the quiet. It was as if the nineteenth century—indeed, all the past—were in hiding and feared to give itself away. The whole world of the Jews in Central Europe looked outward with the saddest eyes. What could *I* do? I tried my best. I was working for the Jewish Agency, and had just come from two years in Palestine, in the desert, and thought that my responsibility was to save the Jews of Europe. Like all young men, I was full of speeches that I could not deliver. Somehow, I imagined that the art scheme would be everything. I have since forgiven myself.

Visions of the Jews in the forests, in green pine valleys as sharp as chevrons, in villages marked by silent white ribbons of wood smoke, never left me as I undertook to master the intricacies of the London social season. I cannot remember when I have enjoyed myself more. Sometimes I became as lost and trusting as my hosts, and, even when I did not, the contrast between the Eastern European *Heimat* and the drawing rooms of modern London was incalculably enlivening. I was suspended between two dreamworlds.

Just before Christmas, that time in all capitals when the city flares most brightly, I was oppressed with invitations. I had a blue pad upon which I listed my engagements, and one terrible, lovely week it had sixteen entries. I met so many dukes, duchesses, M.P.s, industrialists, and academics that my eyes began to cross. But we had begun to succeed in hammering out a network for art sales, and I was confident and happy.

Then a magical power in the Jewish Agency must have decided that these several score dinners had made me into a diplomat, for I received an invitation to a dinner party on the twenty-first at the house of the most eminent Jew in all the British Empire. Only that summer, I had scrubbed pots, guarded at night, and lived in a tent, in a collective settlement in the Negev. Now I ballooned with pride. The entire seventeenth century could not have produced enough frills to clothe the heavy monster of my pomposity. Sure that all my troubles were over forever, I spent every bit of my money on the most beautiful three-piece suit in London. When the tailor—who was himself a knight—heard where I was going, he set his men to work, and they finished it in three days. London became, for me, the set of a joyous light opera.

*   *   *

On the night of the twentieth, just twenty-four hours before what I assumed would be my apotheosis (it was said that the Prime Minister would be there, and I imagined myself declaring to him a leaden diplomatic précis along the lines of the Magna Carta or the Treaty of Vienna), I had yet another engagement, this one at the house of a Jewish art dealer whom I had recently regarded as a big fish. I was so overconfident that I left my hotel without his address, thinking that I would manage to find it anyway, since I knew its approximate location in Chelsea.

I was due at six-thirty. For an hour and a half I rushed through Chelsea in this direction and that, trying to find the house. Everyone, it seemed, was having a dinner party, and all the buildings looked alike. When, finally, I arrived at the right square, I stood in a little park and stared at the house. It was five stories tall and it was lit like a theater. Through the sparkling windows came firelight, candlelight, and glimpses of enormous chandeliers—while the snow fell as if in time to sad and troubling music. Red and disheveled from running about, I stood in my splendid suit, frightened to go in. In that square, the coal smoke was coiling about like a great menagerie of airborne snakes, and occasionally it caught me and choked me in its unbearable fumes. But I remember it with fondness, because it was the smell of Europe in the winter; and, though it was devilish and foul, it seemed to say that, underneath everything, another world was at work, that the last century was alive in its clumsiness and warmth, signaling that all was well and that great contexts remained unbroken.

I was afraid to go in, because I was so late and because I knew what a fool I had been in judging these people according to the hierarchy in which they believed, and thus underrating them in comparison to the plutocrats of the next night. But I took hold of myself and rang their bell. I heard conversation stop. A servant came to the door. Each of his steps shot through the wood like an X-ray. I was taken upstairs to a magnificent room in which were five tables of well-dressed people completely motionless and silent, like a group of deer surprised by a hunter. Every eye was upon me. Though frightened of fainting, I remained upright and seemingly composed. My host stood to greet me. Then he took me about like a roast, and introduced me to each and every guest, all of whom had a particular smile that can be described only as simultaneously benevolent, sadistic, and amused. I don't know why, but I broke into German, though my German was not the best. They must have been thinking, Who is this strange red-faced German who does not speak his own language well? Or perhaps they thought that I was confused as to my whereabouts. I suppose I was.

Then Herr Dennis, as I called him, took me by the arm and explained that, since they had readjusted the seating in my absence, I (who, the next day, would be waltzing with the Prime Minister) would have to sit at the children's table. It was a very great blow, especially since the poor children were bunched up all by themselves in a little ell of the room that led to the kitchen. I was in no position to protest; in fact, I was, by that time, quite numb.

As he led me, in a daze, toward the children's table, I imagined myself sitting with five or ten infants in bibs, staring down at them as if from a high tower, eating sullenly like a god exiled from Olympus. But when we rounded the corner of the ell, I discovered that the children were adolescents; and their charm arose to envelop me. First, there were four red-headed girl cousins, all in white. They were from thirteen to sixteen; they had between them several hundred million freckles; and they were so disturbed by my sudden arrival that they spent the next half hour swallowing, darting their eyes about, clearing their throats, and adjusting fallen locks of hair. They spoke as seriously as very old theologians, but ever so much more delicately; they pieced together their sentences with great care, the way new skaters skate, and when they finished they breathed in relief, not unlike students of a difficult Oriental language, who must recite in class. At the end of these ordeals, they looked at each other with the split-second glances common to people who are very familiar. Then, there was a boy with dark woolly hair and the peculiarly adolescent animal-lost-out-on-the-heath expression common to young men whose abilities greatly exceed their experience. At my appearance, he lowered his horns, knowing that he was going to spend the rest of the evening bashing himself against a castle wall. I admired his courage; I liked him; I remembered. Next to him was a fat boy who wanted to be an opera singer. He was only fourteen, and when he saw that the threat presented by the woolly-haired boy was neutralized, he went wild with excitement, blooming at the four cousins with a gregariousness of which he had probably never been aware.

I liked these children. They seemed somewhat effete, and sheltered, but I knew that this was because I was used to the adolescents of our collective, who were much older than their years, and that these young people were the products of an ultra-refined system of schooling. I knew that, if protected during this vulnerability, they might emerge with unmatched strength. I had been through the same system, and had seen my schoolmates undergo miraculous transformations. I knew as well that they were destined for a long and terrible war, but, then again, so

were we all. Yes, I liked these children, and I enjoyed the
fact that I had left those years behind.

I have not described everyone at that table. One remains. She was the daughter of my host, the eldest, the
tallest, the most beautiful. Her name was Tamar, and as
I had turned the corner she had seemed to rise in the air
to meet me, while the others were lost in the dark. Tamar
and I had faced one another in a moment of silence that
I will not ever forget. Sometimes, on a windy day, cross-
currented waves in the shallows near a beach will spread
about, trapped in a caldron of bars and brakes, until two
run together face to face and then fall back in shocked
tranquillity. So it was with Tamar. It was as if I had run
right into her. I was breathless, and I believe that she was,
too.

I immediately took command of myself, and did not
look at her. In fact, I studied every face before I studied
hers—black eyes; black hair; her mouth and eyes showing
her youth and strength in the way they were set, in the
way they moved, not ever having been tried or defeated
or abused. She wore a rich white silk blouse that was wonderfully open at the top, and a string of matched pearls.
For a moment, I was convinced that she was in her twenties, but when she smiled I saw a touching thin silver wire
across her upper teeth, and I knew that she was probably
no more than seventeen. She *was* seventeen, soon to be
eighteen, soon to take off the wire, soon (in fact) to become
a nurse with the Eighth Army in Egypt. But at that time
she was just on the verge of becoming a woman, and she
virtually glowed with the fact.

As soon as I saw the wire, I felt as if I could talk with
her in a way that could be managed, and I did. Unlike
the four red-headed cousins, she was fearless and direct.
She laughed out loud without the slightest self-

consciousness, and I felt as if in our conversation we were not speaking but dancing. Perhaps it was because she was so clear of voice, so alert, and so straightforward. She was old enough to parry, and she did, extraordinarily well.

"Tamar is going to Brussels next year," volunteered one of the red-haired girls, in the manner of a handmaiden at court, "to study at the Royal Laboratory for Underzek and Verpen."

"No, no, no," said Tamar. "What you're thinking of, Hannah, is called the Koninklijk Laboratorium voor Onderzoek van Voorwerpen van Kunst en Wetenschap, and it's in The Hague." She glided over the minefield of Dutch words without hesitation and in a perfect accent.

"Does Tamar speak Dutch?" I asked, looking right at her.

"Yes," she answered, "Tamar speaks Dutch, because she learnt it at her Dutch grandmother's knee—Daddy's mother. But," she continued, shaking a finger gently at Hannah, though really speaking to me, "I'm going to Brussels, to study restoration at the Institut Central des Beaux-Arts, or, if Fascism flies out the window in Italy between now and next year, to the Istituto Nazionale per il Restauro, in Rome."

When she realized that her recitation of the names of these formidable institutes, each in its own language, might have seemed ostentatious, she blushed.

Emboldened nearly to giddiness, the fat boy interjected, "We went to Rome. We ate shiski ba there, and the streets are made of water."

"That's *Venice, stupid,*" said one of the red-haired girls. "And what is shiski ba?"

"Shiski ba," answered the fat boy, guilelessly, "is roasted meat on a stick. The Turks sell it in the park."

"Bob," I offered, by way of instruction. A silence followed, during which the poor boy looked at me blankly.

"Richard," he said, sending the four cousins (who knew him well) into a fit of hysteria. Tamar tried not to laugh, because she knew that he hung on her every gesture and word.

To change the subject, I challenged Tamar. "Do you really think," I said, "that you will be able to study on the Continent?"

She shrugged her shoulders and smiled in a way that belied her age. "I'll do the best I can," she answered. "Even if there is a war, it will have an end. I'll still be young, and I'll start again."

My eyes opened at this. I don't know exactly why; perhaps it was that I imagined her in the future and became entranced with the possibility that I might encounter her then—in some faraway place where affection could run unrestrained. But I wanted to steer things away from art, war, and love.

So, while constantly fending off the quixotic charges of the woolly-haired boy (without ever really looking at him), I told a long story about Palestine. Because they were children, more or less, I told them anything I wanted to tell them. Until long after the adults had left for the living room, I spoke of impossible battles between Jews and Bedouins, of feats of endurance which made me reel merely in imagining them, of horses that flew, and golden shafts of light, pillars of fire, miracles here and there, the wonders of spoken Hebrew, and the lions that guarded the banks and post offices of Jerusalem—in short, anything which seemed as if it might be believed.

Tamar alternated between belief and disbelief with the satisfying rhythm of a blade turning back and forth over a whetstone. She was weaving soft acceptance and sparkling disdain together in a tapestry which I feared she would throw right over my head. She did this in a most delicate cross-examination, the object of which was to draw out more of the tale for the sake of the children, to satisfy her own curiosity, to mock me gently, and to continue—by entrapment and release—the feeling we had that, though we were still, we were dancing.

"Why," she asked, "did you not get water from the Bedouins that you captured, if you had already gone without it for ten days?"

"Ah!" I said, holding up my finger in the same way she had done with Hannah. "I was only able to capture them because they themselves had run out of water, and were thirstier than I was. And I did not capture them with a gun but by giving a graphic dissertation on European fountains; they were especially taken with my description of the Diana fountain in Bushy Park, and I believe that they would have followed me anywhere after I told them what goes on in the Place de la Concorde."

"What is it like to be a British Jew in Palestine?" asked Hannah, earnestly, and with such *Weltschmerz* that it was as if an alpine storm cloud had rolled over the table.

"What is it like? It's like being an Italian Negro in Ethiopia, or"—I looked at Tamar—"like living in a continuous production of 'Romeo and Juliet.'" I had meant the allusion to "Romeo and Juliet" to be purely illustrative, but with a life of its own it turned Tamar as red as a throbbing coal, and I, a generation apart, nearly followed suit. I was caught in my own springe, enchanted—yet never really in danger, for not only did her father come to fetch me back into the world of adults but I had run those rapids before, and knew the still and deep water at their end.

I recall exactly how the children were sitting when

I left them, poised to explode in gossip as soon as I had disappeared—it is likely that in my absence I was cut to ribbons by the woolly-haired boy, and perhaps deservedly so. As Tamar's father and I climbed a broad staircase to the library, where we would discuss business, I remembered the opera singer with whom I had once fallen in love. Her voice was like liquid or a jewel. I have not since heard such a beautiful voice. But she was, oddly enough, almost unknown. I went to Covent Garden to find out in what productions she would sing. Her name was Erika, and when I inquired of the old man at the ticket office I found that he, too, was in love with her.

"I'm too old," he said, "and you're too young." I knew that this was true, and I must have looked pained, because he grabbed me through the ticket window and said, "Don't you see, it's much better that way!"

"I see nothing," I said. "If that's better, then I'm sorry to be alive."

"Wait," he said, and laughed. "You'll see. It's sweeter, much sweeter."

I went to the opera that season two dozen times just to see and hear Erika of the liquid voice. I wanted, despite the fact that I was fifteen, to marry her immediately, to run away to Brazil or Argentina, to take her with me to the South Seas, etc., etc., etc. It had been unspeakable torture to watch her on a brilliantly lighted stage, singing in a way that fired up all my emotions.

But by the time I met Tamar, I knew that a lighted stage is often best left untouched, and I knew, further, that all connections are temporary, and, therefore, can be enjoyed in their fullness even after the most insubstantial touch—if only one knows how. I was, that night, in a dream within a dream. I was young again in a room of bright colors and laughter; and all the time the dark image

of a smoky continent called me away and threatened to
tear me apart. I did not know then that there is no contra-
diction in such contradictions; they are made for one another; without them, we would have nothing to lose and
nothing to love.

Tamar was the most lovely girl—and had it not been
for that delicate and slim bit of silver wire, I might not
have known her as well as I did. Her father agreed to the
scheme, but then the scheme collapsed, and the world collapsed soon after. Six years of war. Most of the Jews did
not survive. Most of the paintings did. In six years of war,
there was probably not a day when I did not think of the
time when I had had to sit at the children's table, in a
world of vulnerable beauty. Perhaps things are most beautiful when they are not quite real; when you look upon
a scene as an outsider, and come to possess it in its entirety
and forever; when you live the present with the lucidity
and feeling of memory; when, for want of connection, the
world deepens and becomes art.

Ellis
Island

Pillar of Fire

In January, when the sea is cold and dark, crossing the Atlantic is for the brave. Seen from land during the day, the ocean is forbidding, but it is nearly unimaginable at night in a storm, far north, where the ice tumbles down gray wave troughs like tons of shattered glass.

Our hearts were suspended and we held our breath. We tiptoed around, trying not to make too much noise, so that we would not upset the sea or overturn the ship with a sudden movement. We felt that if we ourselves were silent and orderly, the sea would follow our example, and so mothers repeatedly hushed their children, everyone sat with a peculiar stiffness, and many a conversation was left dangling when the ship rolled way over to one side and paused there as it decided whether or not to return.

The quieter we became, the more the sea grew wild. In nocturnal storms from Iceland to Newfoundland, it seemed as if the world were lit up by the electricity of the sea itself. Snow batted down against the ship's windows, and white dragons leapt into the air as breakers struck the bow. When lightning bombarded the waves through the driving snow, its fractured light illuminated the shadowed snowflakes and made them seem like endless numbers of angels propelled and directed in a dreamlike war.

I was offered money to read prayers, but I refused. The Talmud and the body of prayer, by their own decree, must not be used as a spade to dig in the ground, and, besides, when the ship swayed in storms, reading made me dizzy.

"If you won't read prayers for money," some of the passengers asked, "will you read them for free?"

I told them that I never ask God for anything whatsoever, since I assume that He will give me exactly what He sees fit.

"Isn't there a prayer for those who are lost at sea?" they wanted to know.

"Certainly," I answered. "There are scores. I myself know about a dozen."

"Well then say them!" they screamed.

"No," I said, "I won't." And I didn't.

Somewhere in the North Atlantic we encountered a storm that smashed windows on the upper decks, tore away half the lifeboats, and sent seawater cascading down the companionways. We heard bolts snap and we saw metal beams free themselves from their attachments. The lights went off, and though at times we were nearly upside down in the dark, no one spoke or cried out. We began to think of America, still several days off, as a wild concoction of physical laws where we would have to live permanently on raging seas in the flash of lightning and the swirl of snow. We imagined that if we built houses there, they would blow away, that we would spend our lives holding on as the floor tilted and the lights went out, that America was a place of large dark rooms in which several hundred people lay frightened to death with their eyes as wide as small plates. When suddenly the lights blinked, I saw mo-

mentarily a field of bodies—men in sheepskin coats and
furs, women with shawls over their heads, sleepless children lying perfectly still in imitation of their elders—and
everyone was looking at the ceiling, waiting for the water
to burst through.

But it never did, and during our approach to America
the sea grew calmer and calmer, as if by sailing into the
lee of the continent we profited from its benevolence. The
sea moderated, and the land sent out signs—not doves,
but gulls as white as wave crests, who came to join us days
before our landfall, and followed on vibrating wings that
seemed unsteady but had been strong enough to carry
them, through winter air, across hundreds of miles of sea.
I was sure that I could smell land, until one of the sailors
told me that the land was frozen and I would not be able
to smell it even if I were standing on it. But a day from
port I saw a cloud bank that seemed anchored in place
over all of North America. Only on the sea was the sky
clear, in patches of the palest blue, and the sea itself was
as flat and glassy as oil. Then there was nothing but cold
fog and blasts of the whistle. The officers doubled their
watches, standing outboard on the flying bridge, listening
like hunting dogs or men who are awaiting a miracle. The
first time our blasts were answered, they lifted their binoculars and peered out to sea. They closed their eyes like
symphony conductors and strained after the sound. The
echoing blast came closer and closer, our ship veered
slightly to starboard, and then the many restless passengers on deck were stunned by the sudden appearance of
a huge white warship heading northeast, deliberately seek-
ing the storms that we had labored to leave behind. Black
smoke and sparks flew from its stacks; it was sharp,
steady, and flooded with guns; and it passed us so fast that
we would hardly have known it was there but for the

American flag flying from its stern, warm as fire. As the flag glided by, I thought to myself that it was the first color I had seen in the New World. It ran from us in the sea of white, until it was the size of a rose, and then a pencil stroke; and then it disappeared. I began to search again, as did the watch officers. The water was calm, we were close to shore, and we probed steadily deeper and deeper, looking for color. But everything was white.

We never did see land—because the fog was so thick—but we knew (in perhaps the same way that one knows when a piece of music is coming to a close: by constrictions, emotions, and intuitions) that we had passed the Narrows and were in the harbor. The noise of bells and foghorns made a pattern not unlike the few deductive points from which a surveyor makes a map; a pilot launch had come alongside; broken river ice flowed slowly past the ship. But still, America was not visible. Like the blind, we could only guess, for we could see nothing more than silvery water and white mist.

And then the ship's engines stopped. After several weeks of perpetual racket, we were made to think of Heaven, for as we glided in silence we seemed to be not at sea but in the clouds. During the journey, I had noticed that people cried at different stations. Some had wept as they boarded ship; others as we pulled out to sea; some during the storms; some as we saw the warship with the beautiful banner flying from its stern. And now, after we had put the dangers behind us, some wept as the anchor chains exploded from the ship and arched into the water. For many this sound was like the bones of Europe rattling one last time, and they felt that they were finally released. I didn't, for I had yet to see America, and was not com-

pletely sure that the white clouds, white ships, and flowing
archipelagos of ice and foam were not dreams.

As if by magic, a procession of launches came from
the fog. The water was calm enough for our ship to unload
by lighter. After we had stepped onto the smaller vessels,
our suitcases in our hands, we moved into the low-lying
clouds, engines echoing off the water as if we were moving
in between the walls of a high canyon. Because the Americans on the launch were about twice our size, most of us
thought that we had come into a country of giants, but
I guessed that it was a measure taken to impress us. Indeed, we were impressed by these red-faced, uniformed
Goliaths who spoke over our heads in a strange and difficult language.

The two giants on our launch guided it to Ellis Island,
where we were to be tested and sorted, and either allowed
into America or sent back. When Ellis Island, the "Isle
of Tears," appeared floating in coils of mist, it did not dispel any notions we might have had about dreams, for upon
it were vast domed buildings striped as regularly as coral
snakes, smoking from half a hundred chimneys, and shining hundreds of electric lights from windows, porches, and
doorways. When I stepped off the launch, I found that the
land was covered with new snow up to my knees, except
where paths had been shoveled through it in strange patterns that circled the imposing palaces like spiders' webs.

We entered the largest building, and left our luggage
in a room on the ground floor. Then we went upstairs to
a cathedral-like space in which hundreds of people were
already waiting, having come on the Bremen Line and
docked an hour earlier. We were asked the names of the
countries that we were from, and were made to sit in areas
fenced off according to nationality. The room was a forest
of steel barriers and wooden benches. Two chandeliers as

big as locomotives hung from the vaulted ceiling. When there was no fog, it was said, one could see all of New York through the windows in the north wall. But we were still inside our bale of cotton.

It is hard to describe how pale the light was in that great room. Perhaps because we had been so long on the ocean, we felt that we were still sailing, floating silently toward the end of the bad weather, when clarity of air and view would break upon the wall of windows like a tidal wave. I knew that there was a tremendous noise in the hall, but it seemed quiet, in that the collective voice of the thousand people who were there was like wind or surf. Officials in uniforms of deep blue beckoned for us to come forward, and little by little, after many hours, our numbers lessened as people were led up a long staircase to the examination rooms above. They prayed as they went up. Even had we not had the sense of floating in Heaven, the idea of judgment was implicit in every angle of the place. Some had great difficulty struggling up the stairs, and at the top were led away to be sent back—since the doctors could easily see that their hearts were not strong enough for America. Others bounded up the steps, ready to face anything. Before my turn, I noticed a flash of color ahead of me. In the white room, alive with expectation, a plume of red and gold had flared up like a flame.

What was it? I strained to see. An endless file of immigrants moved slowly on the stairs, but then, as the line progressed, I saw the flash of warm color again—the long and beautiful red-blond hair of a young woman in a group of Norwegian immigrants. There was something so steady about her bravery in ascension that everyone who saw her took courage. As we watched the broken line of her progress, she became our symbol. This was an angel to follow, and follow we did. In fact, I was so impatient to get through and catch up to her that I was merely irritated by the inspections.

In the galleries above, I was taken from room to room and looked over rather carelessly. After lifting my eyelids with a button hook, a young man with a military bearing saw that I had no trachoma. Someone else made me cough and breathe. I had to take off my clothes and turn around several times. In another room, a big fat man asked if I could bend over. "Why?" I asked in turn, thinking that the only reason he wanted to know was because he himself would never be able to do such a thing. "Is it that everyone who comes to America has to be able to bend over?"

"Yes," he said.

"What for?"

"Because when we sing our national anthem, we bend over. Now do it or I'll send you back to Serbia."

"I don't come from Serbia," I protested.

"Exactly," he said. "But if I want to, I can ship you there, so you'd better do as I tell you."

I bent over and was passed on to the next room.

There, a pretty woman with cold eyes asked me if I knew how to read and write.

"Of course," I said.

"What languages?" she asked.

When I replied, "Hebrew, Yiddish, Russian, German, and French—and English, as you can see," she got very suspicious and asked me what I did for a living.

"I write books," I said. Little did I know that in America no one ever believes this, as if all the books that appear are written not by living people, but by hairbrushes, watermelons, and branding irons. She looked at me the way one looks at a madman.

"What kind of books'?" she asked sharply, closing one eye and squinting with the other.

"Stories," I replied pompously, "essays, dissertations on Biblical poetry, political science, et cetera, et cetera, et cetera."

"How can you make a living by doing this?" she inquired, with evident disgust.

"That's very perceptive of you," I said with a broad smile. "I can't."

"Then explain how you manage."

"I can only say," I offered, thinking that maybe, even if her eyes *were* cold, I might still fall in love with her, "that this is one of the unexplained paradoxes which are allowed to thrive because the universe is, on one level, wonderfully disordered."

"Turn around," she commanded. She made a letter on my back with a piece of chalk and motioned for me to leave. "Next!" she shouted.

"What's that for?" I asked, trying to see what she had written.

"Nothing," she said, and pushed me into the hall.

By this time I was elated. I imagined myself in a dressing gown, living in a palace overlooking the forests of Manhattan (which I thought would look like a cross between the Tyrol and the *Berner Oberland*), married to the Norwegian woman, after whom I was chasing as best I could. We would be on the same ferry, I thought. The ferry would burst through the fog, and there, in front of us, would be a magnificent island of fjords, meadows, and castles. Enormous oaks would hang from cliffs over the water; horsemen would gallop from place to place, bearing shields as brightly colored as illuminated manuscripts. And, I thought that I would finally get to see the American Talking Chicken, who, it was believed in my village (why not?), possessed the mildly altruistic trait of sitting down with you just before he was to be cooked, to determine the best recipe. I imagined that such a discussion would be both candid and touching.

I was lost in these speculations when I came to a window which gave out upon the ferry slip. A long, slim boat was getting up steam, and the Norwegians from the Bremen Line were about to go on board. My heart rose just as it had done when I had seen the flash of gold on the stairs. Ten minutes, I thought, and I, too, will be on that boat.

But she was not with them. How could she have been sent back? I had been able to see from several hundred feet away that she was healthy—it was one of her beauties; another was her stature; another was her tentativeness, her gentleness. Is humility out of fashion? Then to hell with fashion. She had humility in the best religious sense, like Rabbi Moritz of Oppenheim. You could feel it, as you could sense her strength, halfway across the room. The ways in which people walk and the expressions on their faces are rich and communicative emblems long neglected except by painters and immigration inspectors. But I am digressing. She did not board the ferry. My elation became apprehension. What would I do alone in Manhattan, in an emerald forest taken from a bookplate? What would I do, alone, with all the perfect weather beyond the cotton?

Though she did not know of my existence, I imagined that abandoning her would be the greatest treachery that had ever been. Am I mad? I asked myself. I've passed the tests. I can now get on the boat and go ashore. How can I risk everything just to stay for the sake of a woman I have seen only once, and who has not seen me at all?

When I reached the point at which those unfortunates who had not passed were shunted into the depths of the Island for further examination or to await an outward-bound steamer, my fear was nearly uncontrollable. But instead of walking to the right and down the stairs, to freedom, I stood at attention before the final judge, closed my eyes, and screamed, "I'm an anarchist!"

I would not have been surprised had I been shot right there, but I was amazed when, motioning me into the dimensionless interior, the judge looked up and said, "I know."

"How do you know?" I asked, as my legs carried me away from him, with many others who had been rejected, down a dim corridor.

"Because it's written on your back," he shouted after me.

I have finally fallen into the cold dark sea, I thought, as we walked for interminable distances in echoing hallways as long as roads. At one point, we passed over a glass-covered bridge, and I saw through the panes that evening had come in blue and gray, and brought with it a delicate snowfall. So began my stay on Ellis Island.

They made us take a shower. We didn't protest, for the water was warm and never-ending. I may have been the only one in the new group of which I had become part who had taken a shower or bath at any time in his life. There were fifty of us. We were supposed to have been men, but I had to blink in the darkness of the shower room to convince myself that I had not been subsumed in a dream of rats and mice. The shaved heads, sunken sparkling eyes, and bodies not unlike the carcasses of devoured fowls, strongly suggested Bruegel's blind, Hogarth's starving, and Bosch's rodents. I was afraid to be naked in their presence, thinking that they might want to gnaw at my limbs. I closed my eyes and tried to enjoy the stream of clear water.

I thought that I had made a dreadful mistake, and that my red-blond Norwegian was already in New York—about to board a train for the interior, or happily sopping up the attentions of rich young Americans who could shoot guns, ride horses, and speak English without an accent, and who were taller than I was by two heads. Besides, what would a Norwegian woman want with a Jew like me? Could I marry her? She was a Christian, but I was not sure of what kind. (Since not a few Christian missionaries sent to our village had always been so terribly eager to tell us about their faith, we had endeavored to remain as ignorant of it as we could possibly be. For me, this policy proved nearly fatal when once in trying to escape a band of rowdies I told them that I was a nun. But that is another story.)

I turned to a consumptive Italian who stood under the next shower. "Excuse me," I said, with Italian inflection. "Are you a Christian?"

"*Certamente!*" he replied, insulted and tremendously satisfied.

"Can you tell me, then, what kind of Christians are Norwegians?"

"Yes," he answered. "No *cristiani* there. *Ci sono pagani.* Devils, them!"

After an hour and a half in the showers (someone had forgotten us, but we thought that it was a custom of the country), we were taken to a white room filled with row upon row of hospital beds. Since we did not have our luggage, and did not know what was going to happen, we lay on the beds, perfectly wide awake and perfectly silent, waiting for the officials. I could see snow swirling in the space next to the windows. Was this America? I wondered if I had not fallen asleep at home and dreamed a new world from my own heart. It was not unpleasant. The sensations were strong and good; I had fallen in love (admittedly, like a madman); and I had a lot of work before me in convincing whoever had to be convinced that I was not an anarchist.

When some bluecoats came in to take us to dinner, we burst out laughing. I think it was the hysteria of the idle poor. Just lying on our beds, with nothing to do, we felt like fools. But we laughed at them, and the more we laughed, the more we laughed—until we rolled off the beds and beat the floor with our fists. The bluecoats just stood there, looking on. They were used to such lunacy, but we weren't. It turned to tears, and with the tears we realized that we were going to be sent back. The bluecoats continued to look on impassively, and when we were all worn out they marched us upstairs to a room where we dined numbly on boiled beef, carrots, soda water, and bread. Several Jews remained in the doorway, discussing something in panic. They had missed the kosher meal. As I stuffed beef into my mouth, I stared at them.

"Come, eat," I said.

"We can't," they answered, "and you shouldn't, either."

I shook my head. "I have a dispensation," I said. This interested them, and they came closer.

"What kind of a dispensation?"

"From the Saromsker Rabbi."

"From who?"

"The Saromsker Rabbi."

They were baffled, but still interested.

"You never heard of Saromsk?"

"No," they said, moving closer to the beef.

"Saromsk," I went on, eating passionately, "is a great

center of our people, in Central Asia. All the Geonim
wanted to go to Saromsk."

"They did?"

"Yes."

"But did they?"

"No."

"So?"

"So, Saromsk is that much holier. Even the Geonim
couldn't get there."

"All right," one of them said. "What kind of dispensation did the Saromsker Rabbi give you?"

"The Saromsker Rabbi," I answered, "told me himself that when one is with devils in hell, in the bottom parts
of purgatory, on a ship at sea, in prison, or in a starving
country, one can eat anything that is proffered, as long
as it isn't *traif* and as long as one makes up for it in the
two following years—by remaining *completely celibate.*"

I could see that they were thinking. "Did he really
say that?" they asked.

"Yes he did," I said, knowing as well as they that
there was no Saromsk, and no Saromsker Rabbi.

"Can you share the dispensation?" (They had not
eaten for several days.)

"Certainly."

How they grunted and groaned as they ate, singing
to themselves, almost davening.

The next morning, we were gathered together and
brought to an examining room in which were judges of
a sort, on a platform, sitting at tables covered with green
felt. I finally got my turn and was about to say in melliflu-
ous English that I had mistakenly been labeled an anarchist. My words were to have been: "I am, sir, a devout
constitutionalist, an advocate of democracy, and a believer

in the processes of social order." I had practiced half the night.

I was surprised yet again, for when I approached the bench I came under a thunderous barrage of questioning, designed, it seemed, to convince anyone that he was either mad or in a dream. My interrogator did not ask my name and did not pause one instant between questions.

"Are you a moron? Are you dumb? Do you have tuberculosis? Do you sing in your sleep? Why did Garibaldi wear a red shirt? Have you been in the army? What was your mother's Christian name? Why have you come here? Do you believe in God? How much money do you have? Where is your sister? Who was Abraham Lincoln? Can you speak English? What is truth?"

At the end of all this, dumbfounded and throbbing, I said, "I am *not* an anarchist."

"Anarchist?"

"Not anarchist."

"Why did you bring up anarchism?"

"They wrote it on my coat," I said, turning to show him the letter. Then I realized that the chalk had worn off. But he had already written "Anarchist."

"What is your name?" he asked.

I swallowed hard. My chest almost imploded, but, as calmly as I could, I said, "Guido da Montefeltro."

"How do you spell that?"

I told him. He wrote it down—very carefully.

For the next two days, we repeated the examinations. At each one, I stated that I was an anarchist, put my finger in my ear, like a pistol, closed my eyes, and pulled the trigger. "What is your name?" they would ask, not needing to be convinced further of my political leanings.

"Gui ! do, da Monte fel ! tro!" I would reply. "The world belongs to the ants!"

Soon they came to know me, but not long after they did, their places would be taken by other judges. However, Guido da Montefeltro, anarchist, was securely recorded in their enormous ledgers. I didn't mind, thinking that when the time came to put the Italian anarchists on the Mediterranean boat they would search for Guido da Montefeltro. Meanwhile, I would wander about the hallways, babbling in Yiddish, and someone would return me to the great room, where I could go through the tests again, say that I was a tailor, and get on the ferry. That was my strategy. To me it seemed straightforward, simple, and direct, and I could see no reason in the world why it would not work.

It snowed for almost a week, and when there was no snow there was fog. I dreamed expansively about my Norwegian woman, and reached a state in which I was oblivious of the fact that I had become an Italian anarchist. Then, earlier than usual one morning, some bluecoats came to our dormitory and read off a list of Italian names, including that of Guido da Montefeltro. All the Italians assembled. This, I assumed, was the moment of reckoning; a steamer was bound for Genoa. The bluecoats counted the names on the list, and counted the Italians. One was missing.

They took away the Italians and made the several hundred of us who were left get up and stand in front of our beds. Chinese, Armenians, Russians, Poles, Jews, and Scandinavians, we were a perfect representation of Asia and Eastern Europe. The bluecoats were puzzled. One of them said that Guido da Montefeltro had probably killed himself during the night. His body would turn up in the harbor. "The door was locked," said another. "Go get

Jack. He's had these peculiars since they came in." While they were getting Jack, they made us say our names. Everything was in order.

Then Jack arrived. "Guido da Montefeltro," they said.

He looked up and down the rows. When he saw me, he said, "C'mon, Guido."

"Who?" I asked. They were already pulling me out. "*Ich bin ah Yid! Ich bin ah Yid!* I am a Jew!" I screamed, to no avail. My scheme seemed to have failed, and now I was going to spend the rest of my life in a jail in Genoa, along with the other Italian anarchists—who weren't anarchists either, but had not been able to understand the questions. However, I was not going to Italy, and there was no steamer for Genoa. It had merely been decreed that the Italian anarchists were to work in the kitchen. So, I worked in the kitchen. I didn't care. In fact, I came to enjoy it. I saw every scene as if it were a fine painting. That, I suppose, is one of the benefits of a life of the mind—when you can turn the kitchen from homeliness into a thing of beauty. With patience, all motion becomes dance; all sound, music; all color, painting.

We had a big iron stove, which stood about three feet off the floor and was constructed like a long open crate, with twenty burners on each side. Because it was winter, they were kept burning day and night, in a pavement of flame. The gas jets were always singing in green, yellow, and blue, and when I tended pots the pure warmth made me very happy. Sometimes I washed baking pans; I brought wine, eggs, and vanilla from storerooms; and after a few days, when they had become used to me, they let me peel hard-boiled eggs. I was told without explanation that this was a great honor.

Mist came in through the windows, and the snow

turned to sleet and rain. The harbor around us steamed like a lake at dawn. I had been in America for two weeks, but I had not seen the land. How fond I became of the enormous, cheery Slavic women who did the cooking. Every evening, they boarded the ferry and returned to the continent. I asked if it were really there, and they laughed, which led me to believe that perhaps it wasn't, and that they themselves were not real. Did the ferry take them into the mist and then disappear? Whatever it did, it would return the next morning with several thousand pounds of Slavic grandmothers, who may have lived only in my imagination but who made me taste sample after sample of their cooking. It was atrocious. But I had to say that it was good—which made them blush like maidens. I began to get fat. I didn't mind this too much, if only because anarchists are always razor thin (a fat anarchist would be absolutely insufferable), with sparkling black eyes. Though I have always wished that they were blue, my eyes are quite brown, and quite soft.

One day, I was ordered to go to the bakery stores and bring back a fifty-pound canister of raspberry filling. I had never been to the sweet room, so I decided to look around—perhaps there would be a few hundred pounds of chocolate, from which I could break off a little piece. The chocolate was in a vault. I put the raspberry filling on my little hand truck, and then realized that something was out of kilter.

There was a little window, through which mist was spilling like a silver waterfall. Directly opposite, across a courtyard in which stood two water towers, was another little window, revealing shelves of bakery stores. To its left was a kitchen just like ours. I had discovered either a twin building or a mirror. I didn't know which. But I decided for a moment that it *was* a mirror, because as I approached the window and peered out I saw a man who looked just like me, staring back. We faced one another for a long time. Then he closed his eyes. I closed my eyes. I opened my eyes. He did, too. We ducked down just at the same time, but he came up after I did.

"I thought that was the *goyisha* kitchen," he said in Yiddish.

"It is," I answered.

"So what are you doing there?"

"By mistake."

"You ought to come here."

"I'd like to," I answered. "How can I?"

"There's a door at the end of the hall on your right. It connects."

"But it's locked."

"Rabbi Koukafka has the key. I'll get him." He disappeared.

Soon, I saw two heads in the other window. Rabbi Koukafka had a voluminous red beard, which made my heart race because it reminded me of the Norwegian woman's red-blond hair.

"So," he said across the gap, "what is a Jew doing in the *goyisha* kitchen?"

"America," I said, and threw my hands up with a gesture of resignation.

"Do you follow the dietary laws?" he asked.

"Of course," I said, trying to look thin by closing my mouth tightly and crossing my eyes. "I haven't eaten for days."

"I'm not supposed to let people through that door," said Rabbi Koukafka, "unless there's a fire."

"By whose authority?"

"The Commissioner's."

"Rabbi."

"What?"

"Did not God command us to observe *Cashrut?*"

"Naturally."

"Whose authority is higher, the Commissioner's, or God's?"

"Ah," he said, about to pull the key from his pocket, "a scholar. But wait a minute. If God wanted the door open, He would open it."

"Rabbi, did God make the ocean?"

"Who else."

"Did He cause ships to be made?"

"Yes."

"And when He wants us to cross the ocean, doesn't He make us get into the ships?"

"Yes, I suppose so, though He could, of course, do it in a multitude of other ways. For example, it is said—"

"But most of the time that's how He does it, true?"

"Yes."

"Now. He caused locks to be made, and He caused keys to be made. And when He wants us to go through locked doors, that means that He wants us to take the key and turn it in the lock. And Rabbi, at the moment, you have the key."

"I'll be right there," he said, "as soon as I wash my hands."

No Italian anarchists worked in the kosher kitchen, but the people who did wondered how I had come to be in their midst, and how I had come to work in the other kitchen in the first place. The story I told them drove Rabbi Koukafka's eyes to the back of his head. Not even the Rambam could have untangled that web, and certainly not Rabbi Koukafka—who, despite certain talents, was not a paragon of wisdom. The more I embroidered, the more their mouths hung open. At the end, all work in the kitchen had stopped. Eggs were overboiling, drumming the bottoms of their pots. A pan full of something was sending up smoke. But when I finished they wouldn't move. I waved my hands in front of their faces, and said, *"Nu?"*

Rabbi Koukafka took hold of himself. "Look," he announced, "it's too complicated. The fact remains, however, that you've been stuck on the Island for several weeks, and for no good reason. I have an appointment with the Assistant Commissioner tomorrow. I will bring you with me, and the matter will be cleared up. In one more night you will be in America. Meanwhile, you can help us here, and sleep on the flour sacks."

That day, I chopped several million carrots. They were fresh and full of sugar, and I knew by this that there had to be land beyond the mist, although I knew as well that one can dream up a perfect carrot. I began to think of how to search for my Norwegian. Perhaps in New York there were select parts of the forests, or small hamlets on the rivers, where the Norwegians lived. Sure that I would be able to find her during my first hour in the city, I sang for most of the night that I spent on the flour sacks.

On the second day, Rabbi Koukafka and the others came at dawn, and we worked very hard. Dinner that night was pot roast with raisins; my job was to sprinkle the raisins over the pot roast as it cooked. It was exhausting work, but I was not tired. At four o'clock, Rabbi Koukafka and I left the kitchen. I walked behind him through many gray corridors and up many steep stairs, half thinking that I would leave Ellis Island, half thinking that I was bound to stay there forever. We came to the offices of the commissioners, and sat down on a bench that ran the length of a narrow waiting room. In the center of this room was a partition of wavy glass through which one could see only colors and rough shapes. When the bluecoats moved, shimmering, down the translucent bars, it was like a wave sweeping across the sea. While we waited for the Assistant Commissioner, Rabbi Koukafka pulled his own beard.

As it got dark and the mist evolved from white through gray and blue to black, the lights came on and the heat came up. We were quite content to wait—at least I was. Every now and then, beyond the glass, a door would open and bluecoats or petitioners would emerge from it and walk down the hall. It was pleasing to observe this little ballet of rich cloudy colors. And the sounds of shoes on the tile, the latch clicking, and the slight rumbling of the glass were also pleasing. Whenever I heard someone, I looked up. One time, the door opened, but whoever had opened it stayed in place, hesitating. I was curious. A bluecoat came from one of the offices and stood just beyond the partition. He raised his right arm near the glass, and I could see that his finger was extended—pointing down the hall. "You're welcome," he said, and moved off to the left. Then the door shut and a cloud of burnished gold and red began to move slowly to the right.

I jumped from my seat and screamed. I am afraid that I startled Rabbi Koukafka quite severely, but at that moment I was not thinking of him. There was no way through the partition, so I followed after the gold and red, knocking at the glass as I went. She stopped and pressed her face up against it. Her hair through that lens was most glorious, but her face was rather distorted. Even so, it was beautiful.

"What it is?" she asked in what I thought was perfect unaccented English, but was really a mesmerizing sing-

song Scandinavian. I didn't know what to say, but I had
to say something.

"You," I said.

"Me? What of me?"

"Are you Norwegian?"

"No," she answered, "*rather* Danish," and moved
away. I followed her and knocked on the glass again.

"Wait," I called, afraid that before we came to the
end of the partition she would disappear forever down
some dark corridor.

"Come to the end, then," she said.

I could hardly believe that she would consent to see
me without something translucent between us. Yet there
she stood, smiling, and the sight of her turned me upside
down, spun me around, and blinded me as if a flare had
burst in front of my eyes on a dark night. I didn't lose control of myself, as I might have done, for she reassured me.

"I saw you on the first day," I declared.

"Yes," she said. "I do remember you. You were looking at me in the big room. I thought you were a lunatic."

"Why have you been here for all these weeks?" I
asked.

"My husband," she answered, "was not here to meet
me, as he was supposed to have been. When the Aid Society found him, he claimed that he had never heard of me,
which makes sense—he is married to another woman
now, and they have a child. I cannot leave the Island until
I can prove that I will not be a burden."

"Oh," I said, not entirely unhappy about the conduct
of her husband.

"Who is that?" she asked.

She meant Rabbi Koukafka, who was at the end of
the hall, yelling at me to come. "Not the Assistant Commissioner!" he screamed. "Not the Assistant Commission-

er, but the Commissioner himself! Come quickly. He who cuts bread in the dark has no fingers."

"That's Rabbi Koukafka. We're going to see the Commissioner. They thought I was an anarchist . . . I'm not. . . . Come with me." She hopped a small barrier that lay between us, and we ran toward Rabbi Koukafka.

"Who is this?" the Rabbi wanted to know. They regarded one another in an incredulous way, perhaps because his beard and her hair were not only the same color, but the same length. I have seen similar respectful regard when a relatively shorn sheep meets a relatively hairy goat.

"I am Elise," she said, as the three of us were herded by a bluecoat into the Commissioner's office. Rabbi Koukafka had come to ask for more chickens; Elise had come because I had asked her; and I had come to be released.

The Commissioner was the biggest man I had ever seen—undoubtedly six feet eight inches tall at the very least, and heavyset: not exactly a stringbean. Each of his fists was bigger than my head, and he held the thick slab of mahogany that formed the top of his desk, as if it were a sheet of onionskin. His mustache was as big as a broom, and his voice was like American thunder. We had no choice but to tell the truth, since his steely blue eyes would have allowed nothing else. Rabbi Koukafka stated his case.

The Commissioner thought for a moment. "How many extra chickens would that be for each monthly accounting, Rabbi?"

"Are these talking chickens?" I interjected.

"Be quiet," said Rabbi Koukafka. "Uh . . . two thousand, more or less."

"And would these chickens be purchased alive or dead?"

"It would have to be dead, sir, since here we have no . . ."

"I understand. Rabbi Koukafka, you may have a thousand extra chickens."

"Every two weeks?"

"Every month." That took care of the chickens. The Commissioner turned to us.

Elise told her story, at the end of which he shook his head. "You must have someone to guarantee your support. That's the law. Don't you know anyone in America?"

"No."

"What about him?" he asked, pointing to me. "How long have you known him?"

"Three weeks," was her answer.

"Would you," the Commissioner asked me, "be willing to be her guarantor?"

"Certainly," I said. "An honor."

"What do you do?"

A long moment passed while I reflected on the fact that the Commissioner's steely blue eyes had softened as he looked at Elise. "I'm a tailor."

"Well, that's fine. You'll find work in ten minutes. But be careful of the sharks on the Battery when you get off the launch. Once you have proof of employment, bring it here. It will serve as a bond. Then this young lady will be free to enter the United States. You understand, Miss," he said to Elise, "that you will not be obligated to this gentleman in any way whatsoever. Rather, he will be obligated to you."

"Rather," said Elise. (*Rather* was her favorite word.

She thought it had about four hundred different mean-
ings.)

"It is settled," stated the Commissioner, sitting back
in his chair.

How simple, how fast, how elegant, I thought. But
there was one more piece of magic that I wanted from this
giant. I asked him about the fog, wanting to know if it was
always this clouded, and if it was possible to see America
from Ellis Island. What I really wanted was for him to
dispel the mist, since he seemed able to do anything that
he desired.

"In January," he told us, "it is usually clear. Lately,
however, we have been having the strangest weather—fog
and snow all the time; hail, thunder. I don't understand
it. But, in answer to your question, of course you can see
America from Ellis Island. In fact, the fog today is just
low-lying. Come, I'll show you."

We followed him from his office to a set of circular
stairs which led into a domed tower. We climbed these
stairs until we reached a little room at the top, where the
Commissioner undid a latch and pushed open a wooden
door.

We saw in front of us an infinite carpet of white fog,
and, above, a translucent sparkling mist and a sky of royal
blue—except for the bluecoats, the first blue that I had
seen in weeks. Then a shiver took hold of me as I saw the
city: a rampart of buildings on a great narrow island, windows reflecting the golden light, towers, bridges that
stretched over the fog like long doubled harps.

"That," said the Commissioner, "is America."

I saw that Elise longed for it far more than she longed
for me. Still, I did not know what might happen, for, as
I had found, things in the New World changed from minute to minute.

We looked down at Ellis Island and saw the peaks of the roofs and the gables projecting from the fog bank. Someone (probably one of the "anarchists") was singing an Italian aria. Smoke came from the kitchen chimneys, and a steamer blasted signals from its main whistle. It was coming with more immigrants, among whom I would probably be when I reached the city. Undoubtedly, though, some of them would be delayed.

The steamer began a volley of whistles, the Commissioner shut the door, we descended, and that day I went to America, intending to become a tailor as quickly as possible so that I could fulfill my responsibility to Elise. For she was the pillar of fire that led me through the tangled ways of Ellis Island.

The Night Class

I boarded the steam ferry *John W. Wadsworth* as the sun was setting. We broke through the fog at tremendous speed and came upon open water, where we saw a golden city rising before us. The reflecting windows of a thousand buildings were a leafy bronze color that crawled slowly upward across the gleaming facades. At the center of this was a searing disc of yellow-white fire captured from aloft. In the New World, I discovered, faithful images of the sun were held up to it in an elaborate and extraordinary mirror—and we, having been told of such things as the Pyramids, the Hanging Gardens, and the Colossus of Rhodes, had never been informed of this wonder. Soon I was to learn that the people of the city itself were unaware of what they were accomplishing. For they were lost in a dreamlike complexity which made lesser cities seem like little mountain towns.

I walked straight into a dark forest littered with flash-

ing lights like wild flowers. A little way in, I put down
my bag and sat on it to rest. I was cold and dizzy. After
all, I had never seen an automobile (except from the ship
when we docked at Hamburg, and I thought that the few
there were horseless wagons rolling downhill), and here
were thousands of them. The buildings were too high for
a European neck, such as mine, trained in one-story villages. I did not know where I was going, but only that
I was hungry, and that I had to become a tailor.

I was approached by a wealthy-looking man. This,
I thought, must be one of the sharks about whom the
Commissioner had warned me. He was dressed in a dark
coat of lustrous wool (in those days, all rich men wore lustrous wool, which came from lustrous sheep); his collar
was of sable; and as he moved diamonds flashed from
within the folds of expensive cloth that swaddled him and
spoke his credentials simultaneously. My determination
was of the highest order. I would not fall under his sway,
and would ignore him completely. I began to sing to myself in Hebrew.

"You must be Irish," he said. "I can always tell
Gaelic when I hear it. It's my native tongue."

I stopped singing, looked away, and resolved not to
answer a single question.

"Cork? No. A Dubliner! A Dubliner, like me. It's
good I stumbled upon you when I did, for if I hadn't,
you'd have stayed as hungry as a wolf for the rest of the
night."

Still, I made no response.

"Cat got your tongue? I know, lad, the trip was
rough. You miss the people at home, and you want to go
right back. I can understand that. It's cold, isn't it? But
it'll get colder in the night. Oh Jesus, will it get cold! At
four o'clock in the mornin', even the Eskimos will be

poundin' on the doors of City Hall, tryin' to get near a fire."

I looked at him in fishlike silence, which only served to goad him into offering me the entire world—if I would speak. He declared that I was deaf and dumb, at which I gave him a piercing look that made him reconsider. Finally, after promising me a job building dams in the forest, and then begging me to favor his friend the Mayor with an interview so that I could take up my post the following day as a mounted policeman in the Park, he was about to give up. He shrugged his shoulders.

I must say that, though I did not believe him for a minute, I was intrigued by his offers; it was cold, and I had no place to go. The instant I opened my mouth, he would realize that I was not an Irishman and that the singing under my breath had not been Gaelic. So I tried a famous trick that I had once attributed falsely to a noted Eastern *Tzaddik* who did not really exist.

As he was leaving, I held up my index finger, cleared my throat, and spoke. "Ah ha!"

"Now that's more like it, man!" he said. "I'm glad to see that you recognize me as a friend. I'm glad to see that we have identical views. And how lucky it is that we share the same politics! As for religion, well, that goes without saying." He went on and on, and somehow he led me into a restaurant. And what a restaurant.

It was so fancy that the diners were made to feel as if the waiters were about to beat them with canes, and I was not allowed to enter until they had put me in half a new suit of clothes. So what, I thought, I'm going to be the guest of the Irishman. I was astounded when I saw that in the middle of the room an entire steer was turning on a spit above a huge bed of glowing coals. Just as I was thinking that I had never seen a steer as big as this, a

waiter came over, pointed to the mammoth sizzling car-
cass, and asked if we would like any of the special roast
rabbit. I'll say it's special, I thought to myself. It must
have weighed at least two tons. After my friend had ordered—by sweeping his hands across the menu in a gesture of victory and acquiescence—and after the waiter had
disappeared into the vast and booming floor of ravenous
merchants in the company of women with wonderfully exposed bosoms, I cleared my throat again, held up a finger,
and (indicating my general pleasure at the surroundings)
said, "Ah, ha!"

"Right!" he answered. "I knew you'd like it. This is
probably exactly what you're accustomed to in Cork. I
mean in Dublin. Right. Dublin. You are obviously from
the upper classes. I can tell by your demearing." As I sur-
veyed the tables that were like fields of green felt, and let
myself drift in the ocean of sounds in the great hollow
room, the waiters brought roast rabbit, rich complicated
side dishes, bottles of whiskey and wine, overflowing tu-
reens, pancakes that were on fire, and crystal glassware
that rang like bells. I was very hungry, and did not notice
immediately that my friend took all my food before I ate
it, examined it as if it were a new baby, and then salted
it profusely. Thus it was always far too salty, even for a
Baltic person who has grown up (as my father used to say)
astride a salted herring. So, I had to quench my thirst.
Wherever I reached—left, right, or center—my hand
closed upon a bottle of whiskey or a bottle of wine. I held
up a crystal flask as if to ask what it was.

"That? Oh. That's called bourbon."

I drank it like water. Soon I was so drunk that I was
kissing the labels. But, still, in answer to the questions of
my host, I said only, "Hmmn," or "Eh?" or "Ah ha!,"
which served best to catapult him into a tintinnabulation

of intoxicating promises, descriptions, and (after he himself had drained a bottle or two) song.

I was, as I learned to say not long afterward, as happy as a clam. The vast restaurant, crackling like a fire under the light and lovely arches spreading above us, became as pleasant as the blue sea around a small boat. I don't know how much time had passed in that paradise when, flying to the outermost reaches of the universe, I cried with joy that I had been right to choose the New World, and then was brought about rather abruptly by the sight of a cleared table, two enormous waiters, and a bill that looked like the yearly accounts of my village. The sight of the huge number at the bottom made me shudder. "Give it to *him*, " I said.

"Who."

The table had been cleared of dishes, and I was the only one sitting there. "He'll be back," I answered, regretting that I was drunk, for although I did not know for sure (never having had anything stronger than that grape juice they serve on the Sabbath), I imagined that in such a condition it would be very difficult to run.

I made them wait as long as possible, during which time I heard the headwaiter say, "It's James Casey, couldn't you see, doing the Irish trick on another Jew." Then I was taken up as if on a wave, and tossed out the door. They had taken my coat, my suitcase, and my money, but I still had my pen, my glasses, my razor, and a small briefcase full of books. And because I was so stuffed and drunk, the cold was not too hard to bear.

I began walking into the north wind, thinking to get to the other side of it, where I thought it might be warm. It was as cold as it had been in Europe—perhaps colder. Still, I was unperturbed. I remembered the tale of Rabbi Legatine, who was thrown from a train window in a blizzard onto the uninhabited steppes. All he had was his book of prayer, some roasted chicken, and a double-weight fur hat. But he survived, because—well, that is another story.

The difficulty of going about in shirtsleeves on a January night in Manhattan is hard to describe. If I had not moved fast, I am sure that I would have frozen to death. No one took notice, for they must have assumed that I was dashing from my rooms or my office to fetch a pitcher of beer or a pot of coffee. I dashed and dashed and dashed, until I discovered that I was running the length of a city as long and slim as a serpent. My efforts in the cold had restored some of my faculties, but I was still stupendously drunk, and my course was somewhat wavering. No place would take me in, not even the Harvard Club. The same man in an apron seemed to be in front of every restaurant door, and he made the same negative sign every time he saw me. I lasted about three minutes in the bars, where, it eventually became clear, one had either to buy something or be Irish.

I wondered why it was that in a vast sea of buildings and warmly heated rooms I could find no shelter. As I loped along, I thought of all the empty chairs in large salons, of the empty marble benches by heated pools, of the warm deserted galleries in lovely museums, and of the millions and millions of unoccupied rooms that lay beyond glass as dark and slick as the glistening back of a black ocean fish. If I would not quickly find shelter, I would die. I knew that I could always commit a crime, for which I would be taken indoors almost immediately and given room and board for a time, but that was no way to inaugurate life in a new country.

I gathered my courage about me, and started to

pound on a huge oaken door. I didn't know where I was, but only that it was the biggest, warmest-looking door I had ever seen. I thought to beg of whoever opened it that I might work in the kitchen and sleep in the storeroom. I decided to bribe him with my fountain pen—a beautiful Swiss instrument of ebony, with gold fittings—so I took it from my case and was holding it in my mouth as I fumbled with the books that were trying to fall to the ground. There I was, pen in mouth, in my shirt, my hands full of books, when a servant appeared, half in livery and half in his underwear.

I couldn't say anything, because the pen was in my mouth. He jumped forward to help me with my spilling case, and, having rescued my books, he said, "Go right in. They've been at it for about an hour and a half, but it's going to be a long night."

"Where are they?" I asked.

"The top floor. They're all here tonight."

"Oh."

"And you'll be glad to know that Martha is with them."

"Oh yes," I said. "What would it be without Martha? She makes things so—how can I say it—so excellent."

"Yes. Excellent is an excellent word, sir."

"Excellent!"

"Very excellent, sir."

I went up the stairs, winding around a large dimly lit well that rose into the darkness for seven or eight stories. As I made my way, I could see stars shining through a skylight. On each level, different musical compositions were being played in unseen rooms. I didn't know if this were a music school, a boardinghouse for string musicians, or a dream, but I ascended in the warmth until, on the top floor, I saw a row of strong lights. There was no sense in hiding on the staircase, so I entered the night class.

In a room that echoed from the upwelling chamber music, about forty men formed a crescent before a raised platform upon which stood a woman who, in the light that glared upon her, seemed to have the proportions of a classical statue. She clasped a yellow shawl about her in Roman fashion. Her shoulders and arms were exposed in a blaze of waxy pink and beige and white. I sat down at an easel, just like everyone else, and rolled up my sleeves the way they had done.

It was easy to understand why no one had noticed me. Their model was hypnotically beautiful, and their teacher, a tall wiry man with a mustache and slanted, almost Oriental eyes, was pacing back and forth in complete control. He was the master, and he knew it. They worked intently, for they dared not shatter the magic of his attention and enthusiasm.

In front of me was a big sketch pad on an easel, a box of charcoals, and a three-quarter view of a goddesslike woman bathed in electric light. This was good for at least a couple of hours, and I decided to try my hand at a sketch. Confident of my invisibility, I calmly opened the box of charcoals and took one out. The instructor, who had had his back to me, wheeled around and said, "We're just about finished with the shawl. Why don't you wait." I put down the smooth stick of charcoal. I was not invisible. In a little while, he said, "All right, Martha, let's try the standing pose with one arm out a bit as if in motion."

"With the shawl?" she asked, expressing what appeared to be apprehension.

"No."

She undid the clasp and the shawl fell about her feet. I had never seen such a ferociously nude woman. I was so astounded, and so drunk, that I gasped and said, "Oh!" I wondered how she felt, standing in full light, unhindered and unrestrained, in front of nearly half a hundred men, as if she had someone with whom to share her apparent mortification. But, apart from that, how wonderfully and extraordinarily beautiful she was, how lovely, how exquisite—how magnetic! Paying no attention to the stares of the other members of the class, I nearly reeled in astonishment. The beauty of a woman's face is magnified and empowered by the free-flowing shape and color of her body in a way that clothing cannot match. I had never known this for sure, since all the nude women that I had seen had been at close quarters and always in the dark. Now I knew. I thought of falling in love with her, but dared not take such a risk. I assumed, as well, that she was betrothed to the teacher, for he was the pacing tiger—the leader of the band. Nor was he angry. He walked over, put his hand on my shoulder, and looked in my eyes—just as if he were a doctor. The rest of the class began to laugh, but he shot them a glance which, had it been prolonged, might have turned them into brass monkeys.

Then he asked quietly, "Have you never seen a woman without clothes?"

"No sir," I answered. "Not in this fashion."

He knew from my accent that I was an immigrant. "When did you come to America?" he asked, cocking his head slightly.

"This evening," I replied.

"And you came to my class? Why did you—oh, I see. It's cold out, isn't it."

"Very cold."

"Well," he said, "America to you now is a big nude woman, and that's just fine. But! You must understand that we approach the subject here as a thing of beauty."

"What else?" I interrupted.

He nodded his head. "Good. Tell me, why do you think we draw from the nude?"

I shrugged in ignorance and looked away.

"I'll tell *you* then. It's very important. And then you can start drawing, and we'll see what you can do. After class, you can sleep in the studio if you'll help to sweep up in the morning. But you'll have to find somewhere else to go as quickly as you can." He paused.

"We draw from the nude," he said, "because the world is full of passionate and confusing colors, all of which can lead us astray. Its forms are so various, its combinations so active, that we often find ourselves in a dissociated dream. We are like that, you see—weak and vulnerable. However," and here he smiled, "there is one thing that we can know—better than landscape, better than the planets, better than mountains or the sea. That is the human form. If you can render it skillfully, you can render anything. Look at her," he said. "She's so beautiful. Have you studied anatomy?"

"No."

"Then take note." And he went on, filling me full of ambition and glory, talking about masses of light and shade, about determining the sway of the body (there was a plumb line, he said, that fell through Martha's ear, her right breast, her hip bone, and her heel), the leading measurements, proportions, the effect of gravity upon the flesh, the subtleties of expression, the motionlessness which held a world of powerful implicit movement, and, above all, the beauty, the holiness, and the Godliness of it.

When he finished, he looked at me with an understanding that I had seen before only in the eyes of the deeply religious, the suffering insane, or children—an

openness through which everything can flow. I shuddered
with inspiration, and took up my tools. For the next two
hours, I exhibited the passion of a great symphony conductor. Whereas the other students worked quietly, touching their own faces now and then as they contemplated
what they had done, I knitted my brows, clenched my
fists, hummed, groaned, and moved my arms in sweeps
of ecstasy. I had never drawn before; I had never contemplated so brazen, dignified, and statuesque a nude; and I
had never been marinated in a quart and a half of whiskey.
The lights shone in gold from under conical tin shades;
the wind outside howled as it had done on the sea and on
the Isle of Tears; and I drew with the fiercest, tenderest,
most genuine emotion. After two hours, when half the students had finished and stood talking by a thundering wood
stove, I sank back and spread my tired arms.

How can I explain what I had drawn? It looked like
an angry dragonfly with huge breasts. Representations of
stars, moons, comets, and great moments of history littered the background. For some reason, the dragonfly was
fitted out with aviator goggles and a broadsword. As I
stared at this peculiarity, the immense pride and satisfaction I had accumulated while creating it began to drain
from me as if I were a tub and someone had pulled my
plug. The instructor glided over. I could see that he
wanted badly to discover a prodigy. He was anticipating
history, and although he was not Jewish (I think), he
looked like a rabbi on Rosh Hashanah.

As he rounded my easel, I smiled weakly with one
side of my mouth. He stopped short as if petrified. The
petrification became disbelief, and then (it seemed) almost
fear. He turned to me and asked, "What did you say your
name was again?"

I was ashamed, and did not want to give my real

name, so I made one up. "Hershey Moshelies," I said, trying to be American, and yet not too American.

He took me by the shoulder (when I was young, everyone always took me by the shoulder—as if it were a banister or a bath rail): "Look, Hershey. You know, you really can't draw." My head sank in despair. "I mean you *really* can't draw." He looked at my work again, and shook his head in dismay. "Hershey, a *cat* can draw better than that."

I walked down the long gallery and looked at the sketches that the others had drawn. I nearly cried, for they had done Martha so much more justice than I had. What was I doing? I asked myself. Where was I, where had I been, when they were intently rendering? I resolved that in whatever I might come to do I would mind the real beauty of things and pay less attention to my own dreams—which is not to say that I intended to abandon them but, rather, to use them in a more disciplined fashion.

I returned to the easel, rolled up my picture, and brought it to the fire. As it burned—sword, stars, comets, and all— I felt as if I had been in America not for a few hours, but for years. In what other country do lessons and beauties arise, strike, and disappear so fast?

While I stayed in the darkness, generating resolutions faster than the fire sparked, the art students clustered about the stove and talked in fast, idiomatic English. As I watched them, I saw that they themselves were a painting, and I guessed that, in seeing it, I was already on my way, although I did not know where. Martha had put on her shawl and was speaking to them. She seemed to know them quite well. How jealous I was; that is, until they left, a few at a time, and only Martha, the instructor, and I remained in the studio.

Martha sat on the edge of a cot at the side of the room, watching the instructor go to each electric lamp and turn it off. Finally, there was only the rolling red-and-yellow stove-light, and starlight coming in through the ice-covered windows. The instructor moved in shadow as he put on coat and scarf, but Martha remained on the edge of the bed, the shawl having slipped to her lap.

"Good night, Martha," he said, and then vanished into the darkness.

I was hidden deep in the shadows, and I thought that he had forgotten about me. As he opened the door to the hall, a dim square of yellowish light appeared, and then disappeared.

Martha shielded her eyes as if the stove were the sun, and said, "Where are you?"

I moved into the light. The moon had cleared a cliff of dark buildings, and now it silvered all the windows in a blinding glare. I realized that I was shaking. The loft was dancing in firelight, flickering in black, orange, and white. She was only five feet away from me, sitting straight, as white and nude as alabaster.

"Is your name really Hershey Moshelies?" she asked.

"No."

"I didn't think so," she said.

"Why?"

"Because my name isn't really Martha."

Then she held out her hand, and took me into her bed.

A Crooked Stick

In the night class, and afterward as the loft had danced before my eyes in stove-light, I had forgotten the cold on the street. Though in Martha's warm bed I had no need to think of the frigid January lying in wait outside the ice-covered windows, perhaps it was in the back of my mind.

At seven, she jumped out of bed and began a ritual of washing, looking, and the application of mysterious creams and oils, which she applied not only with her hands but with towels, cotton, little brushes, and strange womanly pompadores, none of which I had ever seen before that morning. "What are these pompadores and things?" I asked. She refused to answer, because either she was too absorbed in the daubing and stroking, or she could not believe that I did not know, or she didn't want me to know. I have never been able to fathom the uses and complexities of the little tubes, jars, cylindrical brushes, Arabian tools, and Oriental implements that women use, and I imagine that it is because they do not actually make any sense whatsoever.

By eight, she was pulling herself into a fortress of clothing that she would have to dismantle an hour later when she started work at the Brooklyn Academy of Fine Arts ("What is Brooklyn?" I asked) as the figure upon which would be based the realization of a five-ton marble statue entitled "Liberty in the New World." As she laced up her boots, she spoke at triple speed of how difficult it was to be a nude model. No one knew her name—her *real* name—she said, just as no one knew mine. She made a lot of money, and it was all in the bank, waiting out the few years until she would return to Ohio as a rich woman, the honor of her family. Her eyes said that she would never go back, ever, but I didn't challenge her. I merely asked about Ohio, and was told that it was the place in America which produced the majority of fine-arts models. I believed her, and, as I learned later, it was true.

She left at a run. Her footsteps on the stairs went round and round and down and down, as if she were running on a corkscrew, until a door slammed in a miracle of banging glass which did not break, and I was left alone in the studio, sitting on the bed. The stove had gone out, and when the wind rose to match the morning industry of the city's six million hands, I decided to fling myself onto the street as Martha had done. To be flung out or to fling oneself out of doors seemed to be the pattern of daily life in this country.

But before I could jump through the lintels, the caretaker arrived and put me to work with a broom. He took me by the shoulder (I was so sick of that already that I almost punched him) and volunteered to get me a job. I didn't understand his eagerness to help me, and he was vague about what I was going to do, but I was grateful nonetheless. He used the telephone to call his cousin, who was going to get me the job. I had never seen a telephone, or, in fact, heard of one (we were cut off from many modernisms; my education had been strictly rabbinic, and then, after I went my own way, classical). When he began to scream at the box on the wall, standing right up against it, I could not decide if he were a lunatic or if I didn't know something that perhaps I should have known. After he was done, I asked him if the machine on the wall was a talking telegraph.

"No," he said sarcastically. "It's a pepper grinder."

"Then, then why," I asked sheepishly, pointing at it, "why did you talk to it—"

"Him."

"I'm sorry. To him"—I looked at the telephone again—"to him, as if, as if . . . *he* were alive?"

"Talked to what?"

"To him," I said, indicating the telephone.

"To *he*," said the caretaker authoritatively.

"To *he*," I repeated.

"I didn't talk to he. Do you think I talked to he? You must be imagining things."

"I apologize," I said, and started to back off.

"Apologize to he," said the caretaker.

I made a low bow to the telephone, and went to sit quietly by the window.

After a short time, the cousin (who said that his name was Herman Lerker) came in, carrying a wool jacket for me to wear. The two men exchanged a few words, and we were off. We ran down the stairs and hit the street at a fast trot, just the way I wanted. Everything was alive with morning, and I saw for the first time that the city was blue and gray. The colors and textures of the building stone were unfamiliar, like a new kind of cloth that one has never before seen, and the light was magically cold and revealing, so that paintings, prints, and drawings were suggested at every turn. For the city held winter like an armature, and was filled with the subtle and reluctant beauties of commercial civilization—that is, color, form, and movement which innocently combine only to rear up like a lashing wave. I was impressed, too, by the health of the horses. Never had I seen such full-bodied, shiny-coated, sweet-faced animals. (They flicked their thick brown tails like buggy whips.) I was told that we were to join a street crew in Brooklyn, and that I was to be an assistant fire tender.

It was snowing in Brooklyn—a fitting expression of the easy silence that clasps the borough and contains it like a crystal palace. We traveled along a tree-lined street bordered by fields and gardens; the trees were young and yellow and beginning to accumulate dry snow in a thicket of arches. As the snow began to swirl in occasional half-hearted squalls, one could not see far in any direction, and I was reminded of Rabbi Legatine. I hadn't eaten, and was still giddy with amazement from the night before, but I was ready to work, to redeem Elise from the Island.

We came to a line of wagons and construction machinery. Twenty or thirty men were using pick and shovel a little way down the street, now visible, now whited out by the snowfall, I was taken inside a tarpaper shed mounted on a wagon. There, I met the crew boss.

"Absolutely perfect," he said when he saw me. "Couldn't weigh more than a hundred and twenty pounds, and he looks strong, too." I didn't know what he was talking about; nor did I understand English measures; but I was delighted to receive a compliment. "What's your name?" he asked, ready to enter into a tattered logbook whatever words I spoke.

Rabbi Koukafka had said that Jews were not wanted for manual labor. Furthermore, I had had outstanding luck as Guido da Montefeltro and as Hershey Moshelies. I thought that the unfamiliar tumult in which I found myself required an active defense, at least in the beginning, since, for me, America was a dreamworld. And I had customarily (perhaps habitually) been willing to do my share in the nurturing of confusions. Therefore, I thought for a while, and (with what I assumed was deceptive nonchalance) arrived at a name for a heroic and dependable American worker.

"Whiting Tatoon," I said, staring toward the blue Pacific. (Actually, I was staring toward the gray Sheepshead Bay.) The crew boss wrote it down.

"Okay, Herman," he said. "Take Whiting out and show him what to do."

I was introduced to several men in the snow.

"This is Whiting Tatoon," Herman said. "Our new fire rider."

"Pleased to meet you, Whiting," declared one of the men.

"Hello, Tatoon," said another.

I was very proud. In the blink of an eye, I had become Whiting Tatoon, fire rider (whatever that was). If only my family had been alive, and I could have written to them. I pictured myself returning to Ellis Island and being announced to the Commissioner: "Whiting Tatoon, fire rider, is here." I was then led to a stupendous machine, the function of which I could not discern.

A steel ring roughly ten feet across formed a base for three graceful legs supporting a tall cylindrical tank about twenty-five feet high. Projecting from the bottom of the tank were six evenly spaced nozzles. I climbed an attached ladder to a platform facing a maze of dials, levers, and valve handles. Herman took about an hour to teach me how to operate this machine. Its function was to melt the frozen roads so that the crews could dig them up. I was told that when everything went right the machine could do several miles a day. I had only to make sure that I made the road hot enough, but that I did not boil it, for then the mud and macadam would run right off the shovels. "How does it move?" I asked.

"You drive it," said Herman. "That's why you have to be light. It won't go with a heavy man."

As I was about to start it up and begin work, I saw Herman running away. I called out to him and asked where he was going.

He turned and yelled, "Just don't let it explode."

It looked dependable enough. The pressure was up. The gas/fluid mixture was balanced. The valves were clear. I sparked the primer flame and fired each of the six jets. At first they came on gently and burned comfortably orange. Before moving the main throttle, I strapped myself to the platform and leaned out like a window-cleaner. Then I moved the main lever, and the fire swelled into plumes several feet long. The lever was only on two, but it could have been pushed to ten. Even at two, I had to take off my jacket and my shirt. The heat rose past me as if I were standing upside down in a waterfall of flame. I moved the lever to five. The fire roared. Almost as tall as a man, the plumes were white and silver inside, yellow on the outside. They sounded like a storm at sea, and the pavement below them was boiling.

When the lever reached seven, the steel ring left the ground and the entire machine became as light and delicate as a feather on the wind. With slight shifts of my weight, I could make it go this way or that. If I touched the lever lightly, the plumes roared up and the machine would rise. I wondered what would happen at ten, but contented myself with swaying back and forth over the road in even sweeps, applying a bath of heat so that the men behind me (who seemed intent upon keeping a good space between themselves and the machine) could do their work. After three hours of this, I realized that I had been airborne all the time, that I directed the thing as if by second nature, and that, as long as I was alert to my own movements, there was no danger of tipping over.

We had lunch in the tarpaper shed. The workers were freezing cold, and held their hands around their tea mugs for the warmth. I, on the other hand, sat comfortably by the door, shirt off, drinking ice water. What a job! I wondered why no one else did it, and was grateful for my luck. I couldn't think of anything more exciting or pleasurable than to fly about all day on six plumes of flame, turning, and swaying, and singing in the snow, while I followed a path that I had laid down in my imagination. Why, I asked myself, was this not the most sought-after job in the world? In the shed, the workers looked sullen and mean, and made me feel as if I were a king interrogating the lowliest of his subjects, saying, "Why won't you be a king? I'm a king, and I love it. Why aren't *you* a king?" They didn't want to talk about it because, indeed, they were afraid to be fire riders.

Of what were they afraid? Did they fear that the machine might explode? That it would tip and crash? That they might be tempted to move the lever to ten and soar into the sky? In questioning them, and by intuition, I discovered that although they feared all these things, they were most afraid of the *fire itself.*

Somehow, perhaps through accident or ignorance, I was not. I loved to drive that machine, and I can still feel it roaring and swaying. I was the fire rider, the one who directed the flame, the man who flew. It was a good lesson, and I enjoyed it immensely.

I am glad that I enjoyed it immensely, for it did not last long. We got back to work after lunch. I repressurized the apparatus and started it up. Lifting slowly off the ground, I discovered that I felt extraordinarily at ease. I could maneuver it with the utmost precision. I could even make it dance. For an hour or two, I heated up the road just as I had done in the morning, but then we came to a crossroads of cobbles. The men would have to pry these up, and all I had to do was fly over them once or twice to melt the ice between the cracks. As soon as I had done this, I turned the corner onto a wide snow-covered street. I was alone, and had to wait twenty minutes for the others, so I flew down the road. How easy it was! I pushed the lever to eight, and sped along five feet above the ground, as fast as an express train. Tilted forward slightly, the ma-

chine was as steady as a stone pier. I moved the lever to
ten.

The machine exploded with a crack and a roar. My
head bent back from the acceleration. Wind and snow
blinded me, and then I saw that I was flying above fields,
trees, and houses. As I passed over a skating pond, the
children fled in all directions. (What a pity that I frightened them.) I was sorry that I had ruined such a wonderful device, and sorrier still that my career as Whiting Tatoon, fire rider, was over. But perhaps it was for the best,
as I next found myself in a place of such strange and yet
familiar beauty that it was (in its way) a balance for having
ridden fire.

I awoke in a snow-covered garden, among many gnarled
and blackened fruit trees lined with ice and powder. This
was so like a Baltic orchard, complete with walls to keep
out the wind, that I was not sure that, after a long drinking
bout, I had not dreamed my trip to America while lying
half conscious among the fruit trees. And the fact that I
do not drink only served to make me suspect that perhaps
I had. Though my face was reddened from the explosion,
I could see no evidence of America. As I tried to get up,
two hands gently pushed me down, and someone said,
"Don't move. We're calling the rabbi."

"Oh God!" I said as I saw my rescuers. They were
Hassidim in round hats and old-style coats. They had
about them a certain animated quality which made me
think that underneath their heavy black clothing they
were made of engines, springs, and rubber. There were
three of them, adolescents with ridiculous silken beards.
Energy glowed from them as if *they* had fire-burned faces,
and when they spoke in their squeaky voices it was like
birds in the morning.

Undoubtedly, I was home again, and had only dreamed of America. "No!" I screamed, and closed my eyes with all the muscles of my face, trying to emulate sleep. "I want to go back!"

"*Meshugah,*" I heard one of them say.

"*Meshugah,*" said the second one.

"*Meshugah,*" confirmed the third. "I hope the rabbi comes fast. *He'll* know what to do."

"What rabbi?" I asked.

"The Saromsker Rabbi," they said proudly. "Rabbi Figaro."

I turned to the three boys. "First of all, " I said, with tremendous authority, "I myself made up the Saromsker Rabbi, when I was on the Island. Secondly, no rabbi in his right mind could be named Figaro."

"Who said," boomed a strange and enormous voice, "that I am in my right mind?" (It was Rabbi Figaro, of Saromsk.) "God can use even a crooked stick, for nothing can make Him fall. I am Rabbi Figaro, of Saromsk. Whether I am in my right mind or not is an uncomfortable question that will have to be deferred. Our sages within the palace are now debating matters of far greater importance. For many weeks they have been considering the question, 'What is laughter?' "

"What is laughter!" echoed the three boys.

"And in the weeks to come they will look into the allegation that children live in a different dimension."

"A different dimension!"

"In the fall, they discovered why bread rises."

"Why bread rises!"

"And, this summer, with the aid of a great glass bell, and an air-pump invented by Rabbi Pupkin, they will find out what fish do at night."

"What fish do at night!"

He turned to the three young men. "Where did this *meshugah* come from?"

"From the sky," answered one of them.

"Do tell!" boomed Rabbi Figaro, in derision.

"Truly, Rabbi, he came flying from clouds. Look. You see our three sets of footprints, then Moishe's going back to get you, and then Moishe's and yours coming here? Do you see any others?"

The Rabbi looked around. His neck was as thick as a bear's, he was barrel-chested, and his eyebrows were like black rugs hanging over the edge of a cliff. "No. Are you sure you did not carry him here?"

"We didn't! We didn't!" they said.

"Maybe a bird dropped him."

"Wait a minute," I protested.

"I didn't mean it that way," said Rabbi Figaro. "I was thinking of a great big bird, as big as the palace, that might have picked you up—just as the fish swallowed Yonah, and just as Rabbi Mocha was carried away by an elephant." (I had heard those stories, of course.)

"What palace?" I asked, since he had mentioned it twice already.

"You're facing the wrong direction."

I turned from the fruit trees and saw a great palace—well, let us say, a small palace—all of brown stone, with leaded windows and slate roofs. Sweet smoke issued from twenty chimneys; lights blazed from within; children in Hassidic dress dashed across catwalks spanning the gaps between high-windowed cupolas; and music drifted down—as Rabbi Figaro pronounced his judgment: "Take this *meshugah* inside. The least we can do is to give him some dinner, since tonight is *Erev Yom haDvorah*. It is an opportune time for him to have fallen from clouds. Who knows? Maybe even a bee brought him."

They took me inside, but not before I had asked what country we were in. Fully expecting to hear a Baltic sound, a waterfall of skinny Cyrillics, I was much relieved to listen to the perfectly balanced vowels and consonants that smoothly make "America." "And where are we?" I inquired.

"In Brooklyn," they answered. "At the palace of the Saromsker Rabbi. Where else?"

As I entered the great hall of the Saromsker palace, every eye was upon me. Although I did not realize it until much later, I was almost completely covered with soot, my hair was bronzed and curled like the hair of a goat, and my eyes glowed from my face like egg whites.

"Who is that!" someone gasped.

"Sh-h-h! That's the *meshugah* from clouds," was the answer.

I had been Guido da Montefeltro, Hershey Moshelies, and Whiting Tatoon. Now I was just plain *Meshugah*, or, at best, The *Meshugah*—the "the" being in my case a title of honor similar to Doctor, Rabbi, or Sire.

Since everyone expected me to be insane (the children grew silent in my presence, and regarded me with shifting eyes), it was hard not to satisfy expectations. Perhaps there is that in me very deep which *is* slightly lunatic. In fact, it may be why I had to leave Plotsadika-Chotchki in the first place: I disputed the rabbis' claim that madness is the same as nudity, and was then accused of both. Only in Plotsadika-Chotchki, whose inhabitants are blessed and cursed with a strange motility of mind, could someone stand fully clothed and be accused of nudity. I had on long underwear, a heavy winter suit, my warm topcoat, fur boots, gloves, a scarf that nearly obscured my face, and a hat past which I could hardly see. "We have concluded that you are nude," pronounced the representative of the Rabbinical Court, as my two eyes peered out of a mass of wool in which I was practically entombed. But that is a different story.

In the palace of the Saromskers, all I had to do to confirm their suspicions was to clear my throat when asked a question, laugh at an inappropriate time, move awkwardly, roll my eyes, or say something disconnected. For example, a kindly matron with two front teeth that pointed in opposite directions, like the legs of a briskly walking man, asked me how long I had been in America.

"I am knee-deep in the intense light of blazing fruit," was my answer.

"I don't understand," she said meekly.

"Of course not. You know nothing of the strange rhythm of blue adults."

"Oh," she said, moving away, "please excuse me. I must tend the gefilte fish."

"Yes," I replied. "Do go to him. They are such delicate creatures, and they give you everything they've got. It's a *mitzvah,* you know, to rub them all over with salad oil."

This was a good game—the price of my dinner in that excellent place.

How joyful it is to discover a really enormous room. They are, certainly, a mark of civilization—their widening proportions quietly draw out the soul, and the dark and gentle borders which agitate and swirl beyond one's sight allow a scrupulous, shielded, infinite perspective. No wonder cathedrals and great churches are built to be silent and airy. For us, the Jews, the great rooms were mainly of the imagination, of longing, though some actually did exist—examination halls, libraries, and houses of assembly. They were comparatively small, but the borders of darkness within them were able to strike up conversations with infinity. So with the great hall of the Saromsker Rabbi. Everyone was there, in an architect's dream, a Renaissance canvas through which glances shot in a hundred directions and random motion balanced out in satisfying symmetries.

"The bee!" screamed the Saromsker Rabbi, Rabbi Figaro, a genuine *meshugah* himself, perched halfway up the wall upon a little platform draped with gold-embroidered red velvet. "God bless the bee! I will tell you why, and then we shall feast and dance in his honor.

"The bee hardly ever rests; but when he does it is with a humble, puzzled look which seems to say, 'I was almost sure I had more to do.' The bee is a peaceful, efficient machine, a carrier of great heavy buckets on hanging airborne legs.

"Rabbi Texeira, who was very holy, was a beekeeper. He spent five years digging deep into the ground. Of course, everyone thought he was crazy, especially when he passed four hundred feet, but he kept on digging until, at six hundred feet, he struck a source of endless steam. This he took two years to tame and pipe to the surface. 'So?' the people said. 'What can you do with a hot pipe?' That was in the summer that Rabbi Texeira began to build his much deplored and seldom understood glass house. It took five more years to complete, nearly bankrupted everyone, and, in the end, it covered several large fields. Long before that, however, they had lost hope for Rabbi Texeira of the red beard. After all, his glass house had no floor, and the rainwater flowed in because it was built on a slope. Then Rabbi Texeira planted acres of flowers within it, and, to everyone's amazement, they grew in winter because he heated the house with the steam he had dug. Rabbi Texeira's bees were able to work year round, producing three times as much honey as they had done before. Because bees love work, they were grateful and never stung him, so that he didn't have to dress as a beekeeper. The village sold vast amounts of honey and grew wealthy, and then became even wealthier by selling fresh flowers in the middle of winter. Invalids quickly recovered in the sweet summer air of the glass house, and young men and young women were married there—after falling in love while working together amid the wildflowers as snow fell and blizzards raged outside. So prosperous did the village become, that the Cossacks decided to seize it. One cold day in March, two hundred of them on wet black horses charged from the north, silver swords drawn, icicles on their mustaches. The Jews gathered at the synagogue that they had built in the glass house, held up the Torah, and prepared to die. As they watched the horsemen roll like thunder down the last hill, they said, *'Shma Yisrael, Adonai eloheinu, Adonai echad,'* because they had no weapons and did not know how to fight. Then their hearts raced, the hair on their necks stood as straight as thistles, and they cried and trembled in awe. *Five hundred thousand bees* rose in a yellow-and-black cloud from hundreds of hives, dipped under the walls, and assembled in a solid mass outside. They rolled toward the horsemen, with the sound of ten thousand engines. Two hundred bees would easily have been enough to drive them back. But half a million! Half a million bees were a match for all the armies of Europe assembled together. The Cossacks fled in terror. When word of what had happened reached the Czar, he realized that this small village had become the military center of the world, and from then on they were allowed to live in perfect peace and tranquillity. The village grew as Jews fleeing pogroms came for shelter, and soon it became a small autonomous republic. Rabbi Texeira, instead of being a king, simply tended his bees, picked flowers, and made sure that the children were acquainted with the early history of the place.

"Rabbi Nachman, on the other hand, was afraid of bees, and used to hide in a butter churn from May to September. It didn't take very long for him to lose his mind: the churn was small, dark, and hot, and it smelled of old butter. One August, as Rabbi Nachman was suffering intensely and looking forward to emerging in September (when the air was relatively bee free), he had a dream. He had many strange dreams—as a man might if his knees touched his shoulders from May to September—but this one was a revelation. In it he was taken to Heaven in his butter churn and rolled up to the feet of God. God was very angry, and, like a turtle, Rabbi Nachman hid deep inside the butter churn. 'Do you think that I couldn't get you out of there if I wanted to?' asked God, terribly irritated. Rabbi Nachman was afraid to answer. 'It would be so easy. I wouldn't even have to break it open. All I'd have to do would be to put a thousand bees in it, just like that.'

"Rabbi Nachman shuddered.

" 'All right. Stay there. Why are you afraid? Don't you like music?'

" 'Yes,' peeped Rabbi Nachman, from deep inside the churn. 'I like music.'

" 'Don't you like humor?'

" 'Yes,' peeped Rabbi Nachman. 'As a youth, I was fond of humorous circumstances. I particularly liked wry expressions, mistaken identities, and circumstantial confusion.'

" 'So why don't you like bees?'

" 'I don't understand.'

" 'Why don't you like bees?' God shouted, and the world was clapped by thunder.

" 'I hear you, Majesty, I hear you,' said Rabbi Nachman, trembling.

" 'I created bees the same day that I created music and humor. I made it so that bees are the visual manifestation of both. Transcribing symphonies into bees, and vice versa, is most amusing, and a good joke is nothing more than a bee in disguise. Can't you see that?'

" 'I see that, Sire,' answered Rabbi Nachman.

" 'No, you don't,' sighed God. 'I'll have to invent a way.' And then God looked at the churn, which exploded from Rabbi Nachman, its pieces shattering into the silence of the universe. Rabbi Nachman found himself naked at the feet of God, and he had to shield his eyes because the light was too bright. 'Rabbi Nachman,' said God, 'you are now a bee on earth.'

"Suddenly, Rabbi Nachman found himself several feet above a mountain meadow, flying in a hill-hugging ellipse, looking for the brightest flower. He was a bee in Germany, in 1266. At this point, his wife rattled the top of the churn to tell him that it was dinnertime, but not before he felt with magnificent intensity what it is like to be a single living note in music; and to trace lines long ago predetermined in the air; and not before he realized that a coat of yellow-and-black fur, two lantern-like antennae, and buzzing wings are the basic materials of humor. Because . . .

"Anyway, Rabbi Nachman awoke with the fluorescent tracings of a bee's life shining brightly in his eyes. He knew that the bees fly in parodies of the celestial spheres; he knew that their hive dances are religious in intent and have nothing to do with informing other bees of where good flowers are, since all bee flight is solidly predetermined (besides, they can talk); and he knew what a bee feels at the edge of the forest on a perfect summer day in Bavaria in 1266. He came out of his churn, and moved right away to become an apprentice beekeeper.

"And then there is Rabbi Pintchik of Birdislaw, whose daughter Katrina fell in love with a bee. But there are a hundred thousand stories about rabbis and bees, and a million stories about people and bees—about those who have loved and hated them, those who have thought that they were bees, those (such as myself) who were born understanding the bee language, about mistaken identities (they do look alike), heroism in defense of the queen, the art and industry of bees, their devotion to justice, sad stories of persecution, et cetera, et cetera, et cetera.

"I can only say one thing," said Rabbi Figaro in a storm of emotion, "which is, that if there is a child in this room who has trampled a bee under his boot, he should be deeply ashamed. I know that there is such a child. I suggest that he make amends by being good for the rest of his life, and by creating good works—not just for bees; but for people."

Rabbi Figaro climbed down a long ladder to the floor. Every child was silent, because most children have, at one time or another, trampled a bee under their boot; and their parents, too, were full of remorse. When Rabbi Figaro reached the ground, he did a little dance that took just a second, It was a very strange dance indeed. "Enough!" he screamed. "All is forgiven. God bless the bee!"

The men, women, and children fled from the room through a profusion of open doors and passages that led into darkness and up flights of stairs. They disappeared like water which runs down a sluice, leaving me alone to

be confounded by throbbing echoes. Although the men
had gone in one direction and the women in another, they
had vanished through so many doors that I did not know
where to go myself. But then a skinny, bearded young man
with Jewish lost eyes peeked crookedly around a beam and
gestured for me to follow. I hesitated at first, but when
he said, "Come to dance for the honor and blessing of the
Dvorah," I followed, as dizzy as a loon, through a maze
of wooden stairs and hallways so rich with age that you
could have boiled them in a pot and made a delicious
broth. At the end, we emerged into a bright and Oriental
vaulted space washed with milky white light.

Though night had fallen hours before, in this
room—as long and wide as a seagoing ship—the sun
shone through a mosaic of translucent honey-colored tiles.
White rays shot down from a high dome, generating the
fume of light in which a circle of black-coated men danced
under webs of golden chains. To me, they looked like
black bees swarming in a flour mill. The white light was
blinding and full of thunder, as active as surf, laced with
gold, and so thick that the dancers were sometimes lifted
off the floor in its froth.

All these men in round hats or fur hats, beards, and
silken black coats were packed together in the vastness of
the hall as close as the grain in wood. Several hundred
rhythms came from several hundred groups, arms linked,
pressed together—the smell of sesame oil. It was powerful;
a caldron, a crucible, a furnace. And I trembled when I
saw that in the galleries the women were pressed against
the grilles, a thousand or more, pushing as in labor, so that
their extraordinary energy could rise in a straight beam
through the turbulence above them. The dancing was an
engine, drawing light through the eyes of each soul into
a cylinder of tightly bound rays that went up past the

dome. I had heard of this in the East. They used to say
that the great synagogues of Asia were like this. But I had
never seen it.

I do not know how long it lasted, but, in the abbrevi-
ated motions of the dance, I was taken back to my family—who had long since perished—and I was grateful to
God for shattering time and allowing souls to rise and
float in the air like boats upon the water. I could not stay
there, for I had things to do and a promise to keep. However, when I left, I carried the memory of that place as
if it were a diamond in my pocket.

Hava

After passing through many villages in Brooklyn, the trolley came to one of the great Manhattan bridges, and
started up the ramp. The roadways were entirely taken
up by Hassidim. We were nearly floating on a sea of black
coats and fur hats streaming across the bridge, and as far
as one could see tens of thousands of the strictly orthodox
were inching into Manhattan.

"Is it like this every morning?" I asked the conductor.

"I'll say not," he replied. "It's quiet now, almost
dead, because last night they had a feast and danced until
the light. Couldn't you hear? All Brooklyn shook." (I repeated that phrase to myself after he said it: *All Brooklyn
shook.*) "They're tired now, so they walk slowly and pray.
And Rabbi Figaro and his bunch aren't here, either—they're the troublemakers. You should see what it's
like after they've got a good night's sleep. They link
arms—tens of thousands of them—and they *dance* across
the goddam bridge, hopping from one foot to the other.
They block traffic completely, and sometimes they lose

themselves in the dancing and stay up here until noon. The cables stretch and zing, the towers start to bend, and the roadway gets like a rubber whip."

I was not too impressed by this, for I knew that they were wry dancers, entirely capable of shaking a big bridge. With the picture of God opening the Red Sea emblazoned upon their memories, why would they be afraid of falling into a little river?

"The Mayor sometimes comes out here and pleads with them through a megaphone. 'Please, don't do that!' he says, but they just applaud him and continue to dance. What a tactic! They know that he's a politician. Ten thousand people start to cheer him, and he melts like butter, forgetting what he came out to do in the first place. And they send him gifts of honey. They always send honey. I see the trucks in front of City Hall, with bucket brigades of Hassidim conveying the honeypots up to the Mayor's office. They know what they're doing. But, if you ask me, it's a bribe. What I say is that we didn't get rid of Boss Tweed so we could have honeypots, you know what I mean?"

Toward the Manhattan side, some of the Hassidim were awakened by an icy breeze, and started to snap their fingers. And then some of them began to dance, pounding their boots in the snow. But it never caught on, because they were too close to the workplace.

The workplace! That is indeed a strange description, for lower Manhattan was more like a music hall than a place to work, even though they worked from dawn until long after dusk, and they worked hard. But it was all music. There was little in the way of material things, but there was freedom. Everyone was in love with freedom, and it is one abstract quality which, somehow or other, always manages to love you back.

And it was a very holy place, too. So many wise men
and scholars were walking quickly back and forth from
one *shul* to another, that everywhere one looked one wit-
nessed dreadful collisions which led to long Talmudic dis-
putations on who was in the right and who was in the
wrong, and if there were biblical analogies, and what this
or that great rabbi would have said or done, etc., etc., etc.
These would be reported at great length in the papers
under headlines such as, RABBI SIDELMAN OF BREST LI-
TOVSK COLLIDES WITH RABBI BALUGA OF SLOVANIAN
HERMONIA, or, LATEST REPORT ON ZOGBAUM VS. GOR-
DON: WHO TURNED THE CORNER FIRST? Most of the signs
and posters were in Yiddish and Hebrew. And due to the
great number of young women I felt continually buffeted
by explosions of rushing beauty—even as, in passing, the
Orthodox girls averted their eyes the way they had been
taught to do since childhood.

"All right," I said to myself. "I've been in America
for almost a day and a half, and nothing has happened
to me. I've got to find a job, a real job, not one where I
get blown up and shot in an arc over Brooklyn. I know
how to work with my hands, so why shouldn't I? A pen
is not the only thing in the world." I suddenly became very
sentimental about my beautiful ebony and gold pen, but,
after all, in my village I had done a hundred different kinds
of work. I spent six terrible months turning sheep's intes-
tines inside out to make sausage casings. (I will not tell
you where I had to put my hand each time I did this.)
To survive while writing essays and poems I had been
(among other things) an attendant in the house where we
kept our *meshugayim,* a "gypsy" dancer, the one who
looked out for Cossacks (many hours in a tree), a baker's
helper (that was a good job), and a seller of chicken necks
(we used to eat even the feet). I reminded myself not to

take lodgings in back of wherever I might work, but extra money for Elise, should she need it, since I believed that she was destitute.

I soon found myself in front of a bakery. I stopped short, remembering the time I had spent as a baker's helper, remembering the joy of stuffing hot sweet rolls into my mouth, one after another, just like King David, while basking in the heat of the oven, though not actually *in* the oven itself. The bakers used to sing when they prepared the dough; I knew these songs, and had a good voice. I also knew some excellent variations, which my cousin Leib had learned in the Caucasus, that made the bread twist around itself as it baked, forming a great variety of strange Oriental shapes according to how one sang. Before *Shabbat,* I had always sung the Caucasian songs to braid the *hallah.* In America, where they could eat as much *hallah* as could be baked, and where there was as much wheat as was needed for baking it, I thought, this skill might be highly appreciated. I decided to demonstrate to the bakers that I could sing their plain bread into fancy shapes. But, being an intellectual and an entrepreneur, I was not content with simply walking in and offering my services.

When no one was looking, I crept down the stone stairs that led to the bakery, and dashed into the back, where I hid among the sacks of flour. The bakers were busy forming thousands of plain loaves—that I would now tie into knots and coil like snakes. But I had forgotten that I had been scorched and singed in the explosion, and that my clothing was shredded into tatters. Although no one on the streets seemed to notice or care, I looked like a blackened satyr, or, better yet, a roast lamb. My hair was curled, singed, and bronzed. My eyes glowed from my face.

Those fat little bakers, all ten of them, froze and then

trembled when I jumped out from behind the sacks of flour. Some were standing with their hands in dough. They did not move. Some had just pulled their wooden pallets from the ovens. They did not move. Some were bent over. They did not move. When I started to sing my Caucasian songs (which were good, but rather squeaky) and prance about for added drama, they took me for the Devil. Because they were *Galizianers,* they had never heard of singing to bread, since *Galizianers* do not bake like Litvaks (and do not sculpt their bagels).

I thought that they were so moved by my performance that they were transfixed. But when I finished and invited them to inspect their loaves, they stampeded toward the door. Though I called to them, they were gone like a shot. Being an experienced baker's helper, I set out to remove the newly twisted loaves from the ovens before they burned. I had to do the work of ten, so I rushed around like a madman, always with hot bread in my arms. Never had I worked with such speed, and the hot *hallah* pressing against my chest made my heart want to go to sleep.

Finishing up in a sweat, I sank down on a sack of flour, and slept. A short time later I awoke to find myself within a tight circle of a hundred rabbis, all davening with Torahs held aloft behind them or in their arms. A hundred rabbis together in one place—what an experience! I jumped up in surprise and nearly made them faint, but they kept at it. With so many rabbis about, my first impulse was to ask a question.

"What's all this?" I asked.

"You should know," answered the Chief Rabbi. "You came from Hell to corrupt the bread of the bakers."

"I did not. I came from Brooklyn ['What's the differ-

ence?' screamed someone in the back, before he was eject-
ed], looking for a job."

They all looked at one another. "From Brooklyn,"
they cried with lamentatious wails, thinking that they
would have to move their palaces and congregations to
another borough. "Not Brooklyn!"

I soon convinced them that I was not the Devil, but
the bakers would have nothing to do with me, and I was
quickly out on the street again, still without a job.

It was not so easy. The Lower East Side was not only a
place of wonder, but a confusion, an anarchy, a chaos of
whitened sound. Walking from street to street, I felt as
if I were being carried inside a breaking wave. It was cold,
and the light and motion overwhelmed me in much the
same way that I had been overwhelmed by Elise's coloring, for things that are bright and deep quickly become
my masters and mistresses, and lead me into dreams.

I was standing on Essex Street, warming my hands
by a fire in a trash barrel, when a man tapped my arm.
I thought he wanted to get closer to the fire. But, no, he
waddled up with a proposition. "My name is Barvaz
Gadol," he said in Yiddish. "I'm the foreman of a sewing
loft. This morning, two of our tailors resumed a fight that
had started in Odessa many years before. Each asked that
I dismiss the other. I begged them to forget the quarrel
and go back to work. But they were adamant. The other
was at fault. *He* had to go. So I fired them both. I was
afraid that they would stab one another with scissors—our
scissors are like swords, because we make heavy coats.
You look to me like a tailor. Is that so?"

Naturally, I answered in the affirmative. And, since
I had never held a needle in my hand, I upped the stakes.
"My specialty," I said, "is heavy material—greatcoats,

Alexanders, winter capes, Bornholm hunting frocks, underwear for polar explorers, et cetera, et cetera, et cetera. You see these strong hands?" I held out my hands.

He peered at them. "They don't look so strong to me. How long has it been since you've worked? And how did you get so sooty and shredded? Bornholm hunting frocks?"

"I was in a small explosion—nothing to worry about. The last time I worked as a tailor was before I came to America. I have been staying with the Saromskers."

"The Saromskers! Do you read the holy books?"

"Of course." That, at least, was partially true.

"Then come work for me," he said. "I'll give you a new suit of clothes and a ticket to the baths. You'll be paid well, and you'll have time to study."

I guessed from this that he was desperate for a skilled tailor. "How much time, and when?"

"As much time as you want, whenever you want. I am a religious man."

He did give me a ticket to the baths (they were the perfect union of Rome and Jerusalem, because they were half full of Italians and half full of Jews), and when I had finished bathing he arrived with a new gray suit. I was shaved, bathed, well tailored, and warm. And though I was not a tailor, I was too tired to care.

In the sewing loft, a hundred tailors worked machines and sewed with silver needles, stitching sleeves and binding furs, and singing softly to themselves the quiet Eastern songs that Jewish tailors sometimes sing. Fox pelts were hung from beams, in long, brown, glistening rows between bolts of English cloth and cutting tables where shining steel met fragrant gabardine. I was taken to a bench, as everyone looked up, and tools that I had never seen were put into my hands, as if to mark the reunion of old friends. Barvaz told me what to do. I nodded as if I had understood, and he left. I had sewing implements and pieces of cut cloth: how I was to construct a winter coat out of these things was a considerable mystery.

I looked to my left and saw a little tailor with the face of a goat. He was humming, lost in another world. No wonder; he was blind and worked entirely according to touch. I looked to my right. There, sewing in rhythmic motions which seemed like (and could have been) exercises of the dance, was a beautiful young woman. I swallowed and looked away in puzzlement. She was shockingly beautiful—so much so that I immediately associated her with the stage portrayal of a fictional ideal. Yet such women can be real, they exist in fact, and they deserve a hearing as much as anyone else, for they, too, are flesh and blood. She was the kind of woman who frightens men, because they assume that she is too pretty for them. I, too, might have assumed that, but I was in a tight corner. After the initial shock (through which, I freely admit, I almost did not pass), I paid no heed to her beauty.

"What do you do?" I asked her, in Yiddish, holding up a tray of needles and thread.

"I'm a tailor, just like you," she replied, tentatively offended. "Only I'm called a seamstress."

"No," I said. This made her angry.

"What do you mean, 'no'?"

"I mean, what does *one* do?"

"What does *one* do?" She was now perplexed.

"Yes, what does *one* do?"

"In what circumstance?"

"Here!" I said, pointing to my tools and cloth.

"One sews," she said, warily.

"But I don't know how! Teach me what to do, or they'll fire me."

She went back to her sewing, and then turned to me. "You escaped from someplace," she said bravely.

"I did *not.*"

"You work for a newspaper."

"No."

"Why is there ink on your hand?"

"I have been known," I said, "to touch a pen. But I don't work for a newspaper."

"You're dressed like a lawyer, not a tailor. Why are you here, if you can't do the work?"

"*You,*" I said accusingly, "should be on the stage. Why are *you* here?"

"I have strong ideas about the stage," was her reply. "The stage is vanity and stupidity, and I hope that I am neither vain nor stupid. At the moment, at least, since I don't know English, I'm perfectly happy to do this work."

In less than a minute, we had become enemies. It was horribly frustrating. I studied her from the corner of my eye (which made me seem cross-eyed). She was tall, her arms were long, and her hair was smooth and black—as shiny as the pelt of a seal. Her cheeks were so spacious and her cheekbones so high that when I studied them I thought of mountain snowfields. Her nose was long and straight, her shoulders and breasts finely formed, and her voice was the sort of voice with which the blind fall in love.

"I need a job as a tailor," I explained. "Not permanently—only for a certificate of employment, so that I can get someone off the Island."

"Oh," she said, "I see."

I thought that she would have nothing further to do with me, but it was not long before we had embarked together in a course on tailoring.

She was a good teacher. First, she made me aware
of a lot of unrelated techniques, listing them in a hurry,
demonstrating, and calling for imitation. "That's fine,"
she would say, and go on to the next thing. In this way
I learned how to sit, how to end a stitch, how to thread
needles, how to "lock up" my work, etc., etc. We then
tried a system she devised whereby she would do most of
the work on a coat and I would struggle along on what
she assigned, so that in the end—with me pushing as hard
as I could while she labored twice as much and corrected
my mistakes—we could finish the work of two. I did my
best, but she did most of it. Because of this, I insisted on
giving her my pay.

"How will you eat?" she wanted to know.

"I can go without eating for a few days," I told her.
"I'm like a camel. You must take my wages, since you will
have done the work."

"Nonsense," she said. "I won't take anything. Let's
keep on sewing. If we don't, we won't get it done."

We managed this way during the first afternoon, and
did a passable job. For several days, until I got my certificate, it was much the same. She struggled to do double
the work that she normally did. I helped her as she helped
me.

She was generous without the slightest guile, and I
fell in love with her as I had never fallen in love before.
As she revealed herself to me, her physical beauty paled
in comparison to what she really was. I began to think of
Elise only in terms of paying back the debt I owed her
for guiding me on the Island, and because I had promised.

And then something happened with this woman
(who would not tell me her name, which—I found out
from someone else—was Hava). You must understand
that we are a nation whose most profound respect is for

old men, the *Tzaddikim*—whether they be rabbis, or tailors, or farmers, or whatever. Perhaps it is because they have had the time to live and to study, and that, embodied in them, is what we revere. I have always seen in them the line of my life both forward and backward; I am deeply solicitous of them; they have a special hold on me—as if they were what I really should be, as if I see in them the holiness that one can see in a child, as if each one were my own father, as if they were unnervingly close to God. I don't know. All I do know is that they can easily break my heart.

Hava, you see, with her silver needles flying, bent over the rich and heavy cloth, working intently not for herself but for another, drew from me the reverence and the love that I had known only for the *Tzaddikim*. She became for me, in her justice, a symbol of all that I had loved and all that had ever moved me. Hava, in selflessness, became the recollection of my village, the winters there, the light that came to us suddenly from the clouds when in our frailty we thought only of the dark. Hava became all the beauty of the hart that I had seen, when a little boy, leaping over our house dizzily into the blue. Hava became everything that was good and beautiful. Perhaps one might think this was too much credit for a human soul, and that such splendid attribution could only have led to disillusion. But she was those things, and more, radiant even in qualities of imperfection. With the simplest of actions she elicited from me the deepest emotions. I watched her, with her silver needles flying, working intently—not for herself, but for another.

I did give her my wages. I pressed them into her hand. This turned out not to have been entirely contrary to my self-interest, for although I could not have predicted it,

she took me home with her, since I had no place to sleep
and nothing to eat.

Almost trembling, we wound our way up the stairs
of the tenement in which she lived. My hands were swollen
from needle punctures. All I had had to eat (after eating
far too much the day before) was a twisted bread that I
had taken from the bakers, and five glasses of tea, which
might have made me tremble anyway.

I dreaded the ordeal of family scrutiny. The one time
that I had been taken as the prospective husband in an
arranged marriage (the bride didn't know me; I didn't
know her; I had no choice; I was only sixteen), the girl's
father picked up a chair and tried to smash it over my
head. What could I have done to offend him so? To this
day, I am in ignorance. All I know is that I was dressed
very carefully, my hair was slicked down, and I was wearing my uncle's .25-carat-diamond stickpin. The bride
turned out to have been a sweet blond girl as skinny as
a violin string, but her father went into a rage, screaming,
"Another fat boy! Yet another fat boy! I'll show him!" (I
was almost as slender as his daughter.) As my cousin the
very incompetent matchmaker and I ran from his front
garden, he appeared at the window and fired a dueling pistol at us. But that is another story.

Hava had no family: she lived alone, and had dared
to take me in. Just before she opened the door, she told
me that her parents were still in Russia, and her sister and
her brother-in-law, with whom she had come to America,
were in Milwaukee. For an entire hour, we talked ner-
vously about Milwaukee, although neither of us knew a
single thing about it.

Then she heated some boiled beef with carrots and
celery, and she served not only bread and horseradish but
wine. Across the airshaft was a music school in which a

student quartet was sawing out lovely Viennese *quazerkas*. Even though these students were to real musicians as a chicken is to a nightingale—I thought at first that they were Chinese trying to learn Western scales—the wine that we drank turned them all into Joseph Joachims. I could not have been happier. Everything was going perfectly. Two days in America, I thought, and I am a Drake (I think I meant Duke). It is true that we were in a single cold room in a tenement, but the food was excellent; I had a job (in a way); and there was this woman, Hava, who was searingly, painfully beautiful. As the wine and I told her, she was "a veritable merry-go-round of dizzying attractiveness, numbingly tantalizing, perfectly and smoothly alluring." I was practicing English, and, like every immigrant, I had been hypnotized by polysyllabic Latinates. Nonetheless, she blushed like an adolescent and stared at her plate. After all, she didn't know English.

As she washed the dishes, I swayed back and forth, fodder for the violins. When she finished, she dried her hands and put on some sort of lotion that smelled like roses. Most women let down their hair when they go to bed. Hava did the opposite, and her arms at work became terribly visible, as did the flowing concave arches of her shoulders and neck. The symmetry of this viscous telegraphy, as smooth as silken ribbons, took from me my remaining will and self-possession. I was in the *primum mobile*. Then she pointed at the ceiling.

I wanted to please her, so I too pointed at the ceiling. What did I know. I had read that, in America, the Eskimos rubbed noses.

"Up there," she said.

"Up there," I repeated like an idiot.

"That's where you'll sleep."

I looked up. "On the ceiling?"

For an instant, I imagined that she could, by a single prayer, make me as light as a balloon, so that I would tuck comfortably against the ceiling, there to dream all night of the bed below and its occupant—as inviting as an Alpine meadow in bloom (without the bees).

"No, not on the ceiling, my dear man," she said, with such affection that I would have been willing thereafter to sleep in Hell for her had she desired it. "On the roof, where you will find a tent and a cot. Any"—her Yiddish pronunciation of Annie—"a consumptive who lived across the hall, used it for taking the air."

"Tell me something, Hava. What happened to Any?"

"Poor Any died."

Once again, I cast my eyes to the ceiling. "What about the germs?"

"What are germs?" she asked innocently.

It was a joy to sit on the edge of her bed, close to her, holding her hand in mine, explaining the theory of bacteria and germs—a theory with which, I might add, she was really quite taken. Still, at the end of my dissertation, she pointed to the ceiling.

I stayed on the roof for two hours. It was actually several degrees below zero, and Annie had left only two blankets (no wonder she died). I eventually got so cold that I climbed down the fire escape and knocked on Hava's window. She got up from her bed and turned on the lamp; she was wearing a snow-colored gown.

"What's wrong?" she asked.

I could see through the glass that she was delightfully warm. Her skin was rosy, a color that the Russians call "blood and milk."

I was too cold to answer, so she opened the window and I fell in, crashing onto the floor like a block of ice. Then Hava's true humanity surfaced as she helped me into bed, drew the covers over us, and to banish the chill, embraced me with legs and arms and everything she had. "We have to get up early," she whispered, "so sleep now."

I awoke in the morning with Hava in my arms. Snow had blown in through the open window, and a snowdrift slept at the foot of our bed, just like a white cat.

We soon discovered that splitting the rent in two makes life much easier. And since I was able to shop in the morning, she no longer had to settle for wilted and damaged vegetables, and meat that would have been passed over even by its mother. As a reward for leaving, I received a certificate of employment from Barvaz, who had found a real tailor—an old man of great skill—to sit next to Hava.

When my hands—infected from the needle punctures—healed, I picked up my pen. Within a week, I had written an eloquent plea for the oppressed Jews of Turkestan, and I was paid a great sum (all right, not a great sum but a good sum) by the *Jewish Daily Forward*, which published it under a banner headline. There was a box in the middle of the article, which the editor used to solicit contributions for the Turkestan Emergency Fund. He wrote, "To give to another without reward is the only way to compensate for our mortality, and perhaps the binding principle of this world." At the time, I still was not quite sure of what he meant.

Since I was paid by the word, I had been very careful to make my survey of the conditions in Turkestan not only dramatic but complete. This necessitated not a few interpolations, estimates, and inventions. I was immediately attacked by a lot of sanctimonious literalists whom I led rather easily into a dizzying thicket within the paying pages of the *Forward*, which made them regret that (and wonder if) there was ever such a thing as Turkestan. I had been accused before, even in Russia, of insulting the truth. Some had gone so far as to call me a devious liar. How ridiculous! Truth is not anchored to the ground by driven piles. It can float and take to the air; it is light and lovely and delicate. It is feminine as well as masculine. It is often gentle, and, sometimes, it can even make a fool of itself—but when it does it calls down God (who protects weak creatures), and suddenly its foolishness becomes a blazing, piercing light.

I was soon able to earn a decent living writing for the *Forward.* I bought a vest in which to carry my fountain pen, and a watch chain—although I did not have a watch. I began to study English very hard, and Hava was soon able to work less: from eight until four. When she came home, we would have tea and biscuits and then go to the Jewish turnverein to exercise—she danced and swung Indian clubs, and I took up no-contact boxing. After the turnverein, we would go to the baths, and after that we would go home to read or play chess. At the end of February, we were married in a synagogue on Chrystie Street.

Living together as we had was rather unorthodox. But it had not troubled us, because America never seemed entirely real. For me, America was always very much like a dream. And when New York ties you up in its net, how can you know for sure what is real and what is not?

I suppose I could have gone on that way forever, and left the past to take care of itself. But one morning, in March, I awoke in intense sadness. I had been so busy and so content that I had forgotten Elise. Perhaps it was because I was afraid to return to the Island, fearing that the clouds would once more descend and I would wake up having just come off the boat, with the night class, the palace, and Hava only dreams.

I didn't want that, but I dressed and shaved, tucked

the employment certificate and my fountain pen (the badge of my real profession) in my vest pocket, and set out for Ellis Island, apprehensive that I might never return. In anticipation of being trapped there once again, I ached for Hava. It was a risk that had to be taken. Mainly for Hava's sake, I wanted to be a man who kept his promises—and there is only one way to do that.

The waters of the harbor were translucent and aquamarine; they ran thick with shards of ice and white islands as big as polar bears. Ellis Island lay in the distance, its Byzantine domes and blood-red roofs glowing in the morning sunshine. The sloop in which I sailed was loaded with inspectors, officials, and sacks of mail destined for ships not allowed into port. Having passed through already, I knew the power of the Island and feared that I would be possessed. It is a lair of the deepest emotions, where hope has died and flourished, where those who love one another have been separated forever, where anything that can happen to a soul has happened, all in full view of the Battery. It is like a sinking ship just offshore, watched by those who have landed; a court of the world; a purgatory; the turning place of dreams.

Once I had set foot again on Ellis Island, I knew that I had come to one of God's places, and that those of us who had been there were tied to it forever. I passed through warm kitchens, and halls decorated with signal flags. I went into the great room, and saw the same people still winding through, silently walking up the long stairs, their eyes glistening in gray light. But this time there was no underlying surflike noise. It was totally silent, and I thought I was deaf. They climbed the stairs without a sound; there were no voices; everything was light and cloudy in tones of gray and brown. In that unearthly place, people spoke and nothing came from their mouths.

By the time I reached the hall in front of the Commissioner's office, I felt as if I had never left the Island, and the silence held me deep within its saddened chambers. What a shock, then, when I knocked at the glass and it rattled loudly in my ears.

"Don't knock so loud," said a bluecoat, who had jumped up to get the door. I was awake now, but only half out of the dream. "What do you want?"

He knew that I was not subject to the laws there. I had a pass in my pocket, but I never showed it to anyone, coming or going, since they could tell from your eyes whether or not you were bound to the Island. I asked him about Elise, and if he remembered us.

"How can I remember anyone?" he said with irritation. "Everyone's the same here." But he did take me in to the Commissioner, who—no longer a giant—sat behind his desk just like any other high-level bureaucrat. He received me politely, but I could see that he wanted to be busy. I asked if he remembered the time that we had gone with Elise into the tower to see Manhattan rising over the clouds.

"Of course I do," he said. "She died."

I was struck as if by the blast of a gun at close range, and only through the severest discipline did I manage to press him for the details.

"Not long after you left the Island," he said, "a ship small enough to dock in the launch slip came in out of the fog. It had sailed from Constantinople, under the flag of a well-known shipping house. But something about it struck our inspectors as out of the ordinary—there were only a third as many people on board as usual, and yet these were poor people who normally would have been packed like rice into the steerage. They were bothered as well by the faces of the passengers as they filed off the gangway and headed for the reception hall. Only when all were inside, waiting on the benches, and several collapsed onto the floor—in itself a common occurrence—did the inspectors make the connection with what they had observed beforehand.

"These fellows are smart, you know. They have to pass a rigorous exam. When they figured it out, they acted immediately. Several of them raced to the hospital, and the rest went on board the little steamer. They found exactly what they had expected, but even then it shocked them. Corpses were lying all over the place, next to the barely living bodies of men, women, children, and the sailors themselves—more than five hundred dead and dying. Typhus. The boys at St. George must have been asleep: for, somehow, the ship had passed the quarantine.

"The living were put in isolation, the ship itself taken out to sea and sunk, with all the bodies on it left in place. But to get this done someone had to go on the ship to bring out those who were still alive. The doctors and inspectors asked for volunteers from among those interned or waiting. Several who went aboard and who later cared for the survivors caught the disease and died. I suppose it was in the handling; I don't know about those things. But Elise, that pretty red-haired Danish girl with whom we went into the tower—yes, I remember—was one of them."

Half in a daze, I left the Commissioner's office and went outside the main building. Sitting on the quay in a weak spring sun, I watched the ferry pull in and out a dozen times, and still I was not moved. I could see Manhattan, Brooklyn, the Narrows, and the Island itself. In the silence and tranquillity of one privileged or damned (I did not know which), I watched small ships and lighters bringing to the piers of Ellis Island a flood of new immigrants caught in a dream, people who had left their homes and everything they loved to come to a new world.

Unless they were wiser than I had been, they probably did not know that a new world of new dreams is a fierce and demanding thing, that it takes from you as much as it gives, and that their difficult voyage was far from over—for the city itself is like wild surf, and lessons are hard to learn when one is breathless in a cold and active sea. But they must be learned nevertheless. For hardened hearts and dead souls are left to those who do not understand that we sometimes do grave damage to those whom we love. Hardened hearts and dead souls are left to those who harm an innocent and then do not embark on a life of careful amends.

I was not certain of my responsibility to Elise, for I had fulfilled my promise; I had only delayed. But that was no comfort. I remembered how beautiful she had been, like a rising light, as she had ascended the staircase and helped me to see. And then, watching the hopeful immigrants newly arrived at Ellis Island—one of God's places, I am sure—I realized that part of my life was forever ended. I was no longer one of them, and I, too, was able to cry halting, choking tears, as the dream subsided in favor of what is perhaps the binding principle of this world.

I got home just before Hava returned from the sewing loft. When she came in, it was almost dark. She saw me sitting near the window. What lovely eyes she had in the half light. She lit the lamp, and it came up bright and strong. Hava!